What the critics are saying:

"Shiloh Walker's best novel to date. Adventure, sex, romance, and the eternal battle between good and evil -- what more can you ask for in an erotic story? Unless perhaps it's love, magick, and mystical creatures."

~*Enya Sinclair, Romance Reviews Today*

"A bit different from what I've become accustomed to in erotic romances.... the story itself drove the plot, and kept me reading nonstop. Shiloh Walker fans' will love this story...a well-written fantasy romance with tons of conflict and suspense. ~*Dani Jacquel, Just Erotic Romance Reviews*

Discover for yourself why readers can't get enough of the multiple award-winning publisher Ellora's Cave. Whether you prefer e-books or paperbacks, be sure to visit EC on the web at www.ellorascave.com for an erotic reading experience that will leave you breathless.

www.ellorascave.com

TOUCH OF GYPSY FIRE
An Ellora's Cave Publication, July 2004

Ellora's Cave Publishing, Inc.
PO Box 787
Hudson, OH 44236-0787

ISBN #1-4199-5007-X

ISBN MS Reader (LIT) ISBN # 1-84360-821-9
Other available formats (no ISBNs are assigned):
Adobe (PDF), Rocketbook (RB), Mobipocket (PRC) & HTML

TOUCH OF GYPSY FIRE © 2004 SHILOH WALKER

Edited by *Pamela Campbell*.
Cover art by *Syneca*.

TOUCH OF GYPSY FIRE

Shiloh Walker

To my editor Pam, the Wondrous One.

To my kids Cam and Jess—my world revolves around you two. I love you both.

And to my husband Jerry. My real life fantasy...I love you.

Prologue

A thin haze of smoke hung in the air, rich with the scent of tobacco and ale. A sad-faced harpist played away by the campfire, his gaze distant. Voices were solemn, hushed, while outside the rain fell in a heavy downpour.

In one corner, behind a curtain hung solely for that purpose, a serving wench was servicing a handsome Lieutenant from the city guard. She had considered herself lucky when he had smiled at her. He was clean, he had always tipped well, and he had kind eyes. When he had whispered in her ear, a number of the other girls had given her very evil looks and as he took her hand and led her to the back of the room, she had merrily waggled her fingers at them behind her back. Occasionally, his grunts and moans could be heard out in the main room.

In another corner, one of the guard and his wench didn't bother with the curtain; he merely jerked her skirt up and pulled her down on his rigid cock, grunting and groaning his way to a record finish while the girl faked her way along. Neither of them were particularly clean or choosy. He wanted sex. She wanted money.

Ah, the ambience.

In yet another corner, two men sat, backs to the wall, facing the small crowd that lingered, waiting for the rain to let up. A mug of ale sat untouched in front of the swordsman. Though he slouched in his chair, his entire body was tensed, ready. His face, one unusually pretty considering his trade, was grim. Pale blond hair was secured at his nape, revealing one pierced earlobe, a single blue stud glinting there.

He had a thin upper lip, a full, sensual lower one. His long legs were sprawled out and covered from waist to ankle in tight, form-fitting leather that allowed freedom of movement and light protection.

Across from him sat a gaily dressed gypsy, his bright shirt the color of the sun the towne hadn't seen in nearly a month. His breeches were red, cut full from the waist down to the knee, where they were tucked into high riding boots.

"Old Lita wanted us to pass the word along. She'd like to see Tyriel, while she's able. The lady doesn't have much time left, I fear." His black eyes—gypsy's eyes— were somber, sad. Very unusual for a gypsy.

Aryn had been hoping the gypsy had a message from Tyriel, a message, a plea for help, that she had landed her fine ass in trouble, something...but he barely had time to acknowledge the disappointment. His mouth went grim and tight as he closed his eyes. When he opened them, they were dark with concern, fear and rage as he straightened in his chair. Firelight glinted off the deep blue stone in his ear as he leaned forward.

"Kellen, I haven't seen or heard from Tyriel in nearly a year. We parted ways last winter," Aryn said, a frown darkening his fair face. His voice was low and rough, with the frustration he still felt over their abrupt parting and the gnawing doubt that something was very, very wrong. "She had plans to meet up with the family in Bentyl Faire."

Concern entered Kellen's eyes as Aryn spoke. Staring at the swordsman, the gypsy shook his head, frowning. Aryn closed his eyes and rubbed them with his fingers, suddenly feeling unbelievably weary. "She never showed at Bentyl, or any of the other faires, did she?"

"We haven't seen Tyriel in nearly two years, Aryn, since we saw you both together at the faire in Kenton. Why did you break apart? Everything seemed to be going so well for the both of you."

With a restless shrug, Aryn said, "That's what I thought. We had a solid partnership; people asked for us by name, looked for us." He paused, glancing at his blade, the enchanted one that had once been such a burden. "We hooked up over that hunk of tin — and she helped me learn to be equal to it, not be mastered by the Soul inside it. And we never parted ways. We suited each other." At least until the last day, he thought darkly, grimly remembering that day. She had left one morning after saying some things the night before that had knocked him flat off his feet, storming out of the room before he could take it in. And that night — that night — the one he did not remember clearly. He had Irian to thank for that, he had no doubt. He cursed silently at the sword, a sword that had remained very silent for many months. *Bloody hunk of enchanted metal, I ought to throw you in the fires of Ither Mountain.* Not only had his best friend up and left him, the Soul inside the enchanted sword that had become a companion had ceased talking to him unless there was a job that needed doing.

In the back of his mind, he heard a low, husky chuckle. The most he had heard from Irian in months outside of their work

"So she just left? Didn't say anything other than she'd meet up with us in Bentyl?" Kel raised and lowered his ale without drinking, his black eyes serious and concerned. "If Tyriel had said she was going to meet up with us, she would. Something must have happened."

"And Tyriel being who she is, God only knows what," Aryn said dryly, using humor to cover his very real fear. "Why don't you spread the word through the caravan? I'll ask around and we can meet up in Bentyl. Somebody surely has seen her."

* * * * *

When they met at the Bentyl Faire some six weeks later, it was with grim faces. Nobody had seen or heard from Tyriel in months. Word had come winging in from all the gypsy clans scattered far and wide. Tyriel seemed to have dropped completely out of sight.

And if a gypsy hadn't seen her, then she wasn't around to be seen.

Clad in somber browns, his fair hair secured in a queue at the nape of his neck, Aryn listened as Kel finished talking. Absently shifting the sword harness he wore, Aryn rose and started to pace the confines of the small tent. "Now what?" he asked.

"You don't need to concern yourself, Aryn. We're her family and—"

"Don't." He turned on his heel and advanced on the shorter man, backing him up against the wall. In a low threatening growl, he repeated, "Don't. We were partners for six years; we shed blood together, nearly died saving the other countless times. Anything that concerns Tyriel concerns me. *Everything* that concerns her concerns me."

Not bothering to hide his small, pleased smile, Kel relaxed. "I'd hoped you would say that. Something tells me Tyriel is going to need all the help she can get." Rising, Kel wandered over and picked up his harp, absently strumming a somber tune. "The best thing to do is go back to where you two were when you split, since that seems to be the last time anybody saw her. That seems like the first place we ought to try."

"The first thing we need to do is contact her father," Aryn contradicted, turning to face the suddenly still gypsy.

"Her father."

"Can you think of a person better equipped to find her?" he asked dryly.

"Her father." The forced laughter didn't quite hide the nerves in his eyes as he ran a hand through his short cap of black curls. He offered, "We could just send him a message through the courier guild."

"Since when did gypsies trust the guild?" Aryn asked. "Send one of your own."

"Right." Rubbing his sweaty hands down the sides of his saffron trews, Kel tried to figure out if any of his kin would look upon it as an adventure. After all, how many gypsies got to see the enchanted kingdom?

Thousands, probably, he thought, sighing dramatically. And none lived to tell the tale.

"And maybe we will be lucky. Maybe Tyriel has been with him all this time," Aryn offered, trying to cheer up the younger man.

Not likely though. The elvish kingdoms would drive her mad within a month. Be her father a prince of the elves or no.

* * * * *

Aryn tossed restlessly, tangled in the rough linen sheets. They clung to his naked body, twining around his long muscled limbs like ropes as he fought the scenes playing out inside his head. Trapped in dreams, he flung his arm out and muttered, "Tyriel."

Irian was on the bed beside him. And the metal of the blade was pulsing, glowing a soft, gleaming silver, tinged with red. Enraged.

He could see her.

They could see her.

God, what has happened to her? Aryn thought, hardly able to believe the slumped still figure was the bright laughing woman he had spent six years with.

A sob shimmered in the air and she turned away from the wall, revealing a bruised swollen face and hollow sunken eyes. The light was gone from those eyes and Aryn shuddered at the sheer hopelessness he saw in her face. Impotent rage ripped through him as he saw evidence that she had been abused and raped, viciously. Blood and bruises mottled her thighs, some old, some new. Scars showed on her belly and legs.

Stretching his hand out, he went to her. But mere feet from her, he was stopped in his tracks, unable to go further. Straining against the barrier he couldn't see, Aryn shouted out her name.

It was his own voice that woke him.

Hair, face and torso soaked with sweat, Aryn sat up in the bed, his breath sawing in and out as he scrubbed his gritty eyes. A misty form shimmered into view and a large brooding figure started to pace, his eyes glowing red with rage, echoing the red that still shimmered around the blade. This was Irian, long-dead warrior of the Jiuspu, a primitive, valiant race that had been the progenitors of the gypsies, thousands of years gone from the land.

"Tyriel, what happened?" Aryn muttered, shaking his head as Irian prowled the room, swearing in a language no longer spoken.

"Ah, but the poor lass is going mad, so hurt, so broken. Why did she n' call?" Irian continued to pace as Aryn brooded.

What in the world could have happened between the four weeks between her leaving Ethridge and the Bentyl Faire?

"We will find her. I will help you," Irian swore, his voice low and rough, the primitive power inside of him throttled back. He was reining it in, purposely keeping himself from overwhelming Aryn's mind.

"We?" Aryn asked, tossing the enchanter a look. "Or you, after taking me over?"

"*We. Tyriel is yours, not mine,*" Irian whispered. "*After all, my body is long dead.*" Sadness filled the man's eyes, and grief, and he faded from view, and then a door shut inside Aryn's mind, and the swordsman knew Irian would respond to nothing else.

Even Aryn's response that Tyriel didn't belong to Aryn.

* * * * *

The pain, nauseating as it was, no longer kept her awake. Lost in a tumbling maze of dreams, the pain lashed at her out of the darkness. Flinching, she shrieked and tried to pull away from it, to hide.

But it merely found her again, and tore at her repeatedly.

When the pain did little to jar her out of her daze, the things came. Wet, spongy beasts from the underworld, crawling over her, invading her, ripping and biting at her breasts, her nipples, her thighs, her cleft, until she shrieked with the agony of it. And even though the rape the demons inflicted wasn't real, just illusion, she feared it more than the physical rapes that occurred sporadically.

The things rejoiced in her loathing, in her fear. There had been a time when she would have battled them, banished them as the illusions she knew them to be.

But there had also been a time when she would have lashed out and destroyed the man responsible.

In despair, she curled in on herself, to wait it out. It would fade. It always did.

And it would come again.

It always did.

Chapter One
Six Years Earlier

Gay, cheerful music poured from the flute she held to her lips. Eyes ever watchful, she played on with only a scrap of attention on the music while she studied the crowd in front of her. She kept her hood over her head and her eyes low. In a place such as this, nobody thought twice of such things. Many people here were criminals, thieves, trying to hide themselves. They would think the same of her.

The innkeeper was a slovenly thing, Tyriel thought. But he was no worse than the rest in this city. How had it changed so much? It had only been a few years. Or had it? It was easy enough to lose track of time when you spent so much of it alone.

No longer were men expected to take a wench upstairs. Now they simply retreated to the shadowy corners, engaging in oral sex for the most part, holding the wench by the hair or shoulders, tossing her a few coins when he was done. But one or two over the past few hours had actually pushed the woman up against the wall and fucked her right there.

Since the wenches seemed to enjoy the money, and the attention, Tyriel just turned a blind eye. And a deaf ear when need be. Too bad she couldn't turn her nose off. The scent of unwashed bodies and copious sex, stale beer, burnt food—oh how she longed for the mountains, the plains, the green of the wood.

Her eyes closed and she briefly thought of home, longed for it—not the wagon trains of the gypsies, but home—the Kingdoms of Eivisa, and the sprawling valleys and towering peaks of Averne, her father's realm, to walk among the woods and feel the magick of it seeping into her bones, to lie down on the mossy green grass and feel the hard, powerful body of a warrior over her while the magick mingled and their bodies—

Boisterous shouts intruded on her thoughts and she opened her eyes, torn out of her fantasies.

One lout, in particular, was annoying the hell out of her. He had made a number of lewd comments in her direction the night before, all of which she had brushed off and ignored. But he was already drunk and getting drunker, and the night was still young.

Turning her attention to the rest of the crowd, she dismissed him from her mind and looked for a likely mark with full pockets. The one she found was already nodding happily to her music, a sweet-looking old peddler, prosperous from the looks of it. What in the name of hell he was doing in this dive, she couldn't understand.

And even as she changed her music to match the emotions she sensed in him, he tossed two silver marks into the open case at her feet.

She nodded at him in thanks, pleased. Those two silver marks would let her leave a few days earlier than planned.

And there just might be more where those came from. It wasn't exactly the most honorable way to play, but she was not using magick. Just playing to suit his moods. What he gave was of his own free will.

A few coppers joined the scattered coins in the case but she didn't even notice as a loud crash, followed by a bellow, echoed through the tavern.

The guard, an overgrown hulk of a man, looked at the spreading patch of wine that soaked the front of his already filthy uniform. The serving boy, no older than nine, stood on weak knees, his face pale, too afraid to even dodge the blow that was sure to come.

Behind the bar, the innkeeper did nothing, merely filled mug after mug with the disgusting ale. Her flute landed on the ground before the cup fell from the boy's trembling hands. A growl rumbled low in her throat as she crossed the room quicker than human eyes could follow. Another man was moving, a dark cloaked figure, but Tyriel moved far quicker.

The small boy stared at the guard, pathetically awaiting the blow. But the huge fist never landed. A dark, delicate hand snatched the boy, shoving him backward as the minstrel faced down the guard.

"I doubt anybody is going to notice one more stain on that nasty uniform," she said softly, her husky voice carrying through the suddenly silent inn as she pushed her hood back, revealing masses of raven black curls, dusky skin and topaz eyes. Her wide, mobile mouth, the color of a rose in bloom, curved up in an easy smile that belied the warning in her eyes.

"Mind your own business, bitch," he growled, looming over her, reaching out to knock her aside.

When she stood there, immovable as a rock, the guard fell back slightly. "I told you to butt out," he snarled, placing the flat of his hand on her chest and shoving.

The girl, though nearly as tall as he, was reed slender and should have gone flying through the air. So it came as somewhat of a surprise when he failed to budge her. The mortal fell back, his hand falling from his blade, his eyes narrowed and curious as he watched from the shadows of his hood as the woman smiled tauntingly at the guard.

Backing off, the half-intoxicated guard studied her warily.

Nonchalantly, she reached up to shove her heavy fall of raven curls away from her face and twisted them into a tail, securing it with a leather cord, all the while staring at the guard, that same amused little smile curving her mobile mouth.

"Elf."

"Look there, see the ears? Oh, my stars, see her eyes?"

The voices blended into the background as she took a step closer, one hand straying to her neck, stroking the amulet there.

The mortal shook his head, smiling slightly as he retreated back to his table in the corner.

The guard's eyes, like everyone else's, were riveted on the delicate point of her ears. The luminescent sheen of her eyes intensified and the air around her almost seemed to shimmer. Smiling at him, she asked, "Shall I continue to mind my own business?"

"Perhaps...perhaps it was my own...my own fault, milady," the guard stuttered, fear making his mouth suddenly dry. "An' he is jes' a kid, after all. No harm done."

"None at all." An agreeable smile lit Tyriel's face and the tension that had filled her drained out as the guard backed down, dropping into his seat, studiously avoiding her gaze.

It didn't surprise her, as far south as she was. The folk in Zhalia were notoriously superstitious; elves were ranked on the same level as saints and angels and demons. To be feared, respected, or worshipped, depending who you asked and when.

Though one might think unkindly thoughts of the fae, few spoke them aloud for fear that the fae people would hear and drag them off to the cities in the hills to slave away in the elvish mines.

Though her chest ached from resisting the bully's shove, she didn't reach up to rub it, knowing better than to show any sign of weakness or reaction.

A low amused voice said, "That's a rather...interesting act you have there. What was that, mass hypnosis?"

Turning to study the hooded stranger in the corner, Tyriel cocked her head. "Nothing so extravagant." Moving closer, she bent over the table and gave a conspiratorial wink and said, "We elves eat babies at breakfast, didn't you know? They know better than to anger us."

"Hmm. How odd. All the elves I've ever known were vegetarians," the man said in a low voice, careful to keep anybody else from overhearing as he reached up and shoved his hood back.

Oh, my, Tyriel thought with interest as she studied the pale face revealed. A face that could have been carved from alabaster stared back at her, with wide eyes of deep blue. *My, my, my.*

The slight arch of her brow was the only sign that she was the slightest bit impressed by that little known fact. And nothing revealed that her tongue was about ready to hang out of her mouth. "Are you going to give me away? Let them know how meek and cowardly we really are?"

"I didn't say a thing about meek or cowardly." Gesturing to the seat at his side, he said, "I am curious exactly how you managed that, though. I've never seen a guard from this towne back down from anything short of a fair fight."

"It wouldn't have been fair. I was busting men like him when I was barely old enough to pick up a sword."

"Hardly what I meant."

Recognizing the persistence, Tyriel shrugged. "It's not a secret or anything. The folk in this part of the country are notoriously superstitious. They still believe that we lurk around in the shadow world, waiting for people to displease us so we can haul them away to harvest our mines for us."

"I doubt you'd let somebody who wasn't elvish into your mines," the swordsman said, beckoning for another ale. "Can I buy you one?"

"I'll pass." She shuddered in remembrance of the one taste she had taken as she studied him. And he was quite a treat to the eyes…a fine one, indeed. That mouth…it was giving her some naughty ideas that had her belly getting tight as she shifted on the hard bench. "You seem to know quite a bit about the kin," Tyriel mused, declining the offered mug from the serving girl. "How is that?"

He flashed her a grin. "I get around."

"Hmmm. In your travels, have you heard of glamour?" she asked, her voice dropping to just above a whisper. With a conspiratorial wink, she said, "It's a neat little trick that makes people think they are seeing something that isn't there. Or more than what they already see."

"So your eyes weren't really glowing in the dark?"

"What do you think?" she returned with a smile, the tip of her tongue darting out to wet her lips. When he merely arched a pale gold brow at her, she sighed. "Swordsman, do you really think I would share such secrets with a man I don't know?"

"You saved that boy from a sound beating." His eyes drifted over to the guard who sat staring sullenly into his wine. "The guard will forget by morning, but that wouldn't help the boy. He would have been hurt badly enough to not work for a day or two. If he can't do his job here, he's to be sold."

With a curl of her lip, Tyriel said, "Slaves. That's one of the reasons I head out this week. There was a time when slavery wasn't lawful here. I was shocked to learn it had been legalized."

Her eyes drifted over to where the serving boy hurried back and forth between the kitchen and the tables. Often, he cast grateful eyes her way as he carefully avoided the area around the surly guard. A handsome child, if you could overlook the overly long, tangled hair and obvious malnourishment.

And more than one patron had overlooked. Body slaves were bad enough, but to force a child into that role was unthinkable. And it wouldn't be long before the innkeeper decided to do just that. Tyriel had already noticed the appraising looks the innkeeper gave the boy when a particular customer would stare at him overly long.

"I've only been here a month myself. Hired on for a job. Once the contract is up, I'm northbound." Sympathy darkened his eyes as he watched the boy as well.

Yeah, a handsome child.

At his back, his sword seemed to weigh down heavily on him for just a moment. Automatically, he shifted the harness as he turned his eyes back to the elf. "I'm Aryn. May I ask your name?"

"Tyriel," she murmured, dragging her eyes from the child and studying the outrageously beautiful man in front of her. Over the morass of scents in the inn, she could smell him, and he smelled delicious…warm, male, clean. The sword strapped to his back was harnessed across what looked to be a deliciously powerful chest.

The sword…it drew her eye, flashing far more brightly in the dim light than it should have. The carving in the pommel was scrolled and marked, letters—familiar, they seemed to move and twist, and call—Tyriel shook her head slightly as Aryn shifted his shoulders once more, distracting her, drawing her attention away from the sword's hilt and pommel, and back to him.

His shoulders looked wide and strong and his arms were long, lean and muscled under the clean cotton of his shirt. The sleeves of that shirt were rolled up to his elbows, revealing muscled forearms, thick wrists, long-fingered hands with wide palms. And his smell kept beckoning her. She was getting hotter just staring at him. "Just Tyriel."

A small hand appeared on the swordsman's shoulder. Turning her eyes upward, Tyriel watched as one of the serving girls lowered her lips to speak quietly into his ear. A slow smile tugged at his mouth and he gave a slight nod before turning his attention back to Tyriel.

The girl, well, woman had large breasts, a narrow waist, and full hips. Exceptionally clean, which was unusual in a dive like this. When Tyriel's eyes landed on the brand on her wrist, she fit the pieces together. It was the shape of a quarter-moon, which meant the girl was an indentured servant. She could work off her five years here, or be bought by a willing party and work off the time with another.

If the mark had been an 'X,' it would have meant she was a slave, and freedom was something that would never happen for her. An 'X' encircled meant a body slave, basically a whore who whored for her master and turned the money over to that master. A whore who had no choice in his or her bed partners, or any say in where she bedded that partner. Tyriel had seen body slaves who knelt in alleyways in broad daylight to service or be mounted.

But this serving girl was looking for a new keeper.

She recognized the satisfaction in the serving girl's eyes as she strolled away, hips swaying subtly beneath the plain blue wool of her skirt. With a sigh, Tyriel thought, too bad.

She fought not to let her lip poke out as she squirmed on the seat, the wetness between her thighs seeming to mock her. Damn it all.

* * * * *

Aryn the swordsman at least had the decency to take his tumble upstairs. The girl was clean and soft and sweet-smelling — looking for a way to a better life.

Aryn couldn't, and wasn't interested in, offering that, but a soft female beside him for the night wasn't a bad thing. He'd leave some extra money with her so she could stash it. Most indentured servants skimmed a little bit of money here and there, hoping to earn enough to buy their freedom a year or two sooner.

Barely clearing the door, he turned and grabbed her, pinning her against the wall and lifting her skirt to close his hands over naked hips. "Why, you naughty thing, no undergarments," he purred, nibbling his way down her neck.

She hadn't accepted another man's favor all night, or the past three, waiting for this one. He was clean, he was handsome, and he had kind eyes. Since she did have some say in whom she spread her thighs for, she had waited and watched him.

With a smile, she pulled her linen shift up and over her head, freeing the large breasts that had teased and taunted Aryn half the night. "Not a thing, sirrah," she replied. "I was hopin' you'd like some company after all. And I wanted nothin' in y'way."

It had been nearly four months since Aryn had been able to get to a woman decent enough, clean enough to touch. Without another thought in his mind, he freed his cock, then lifted her and drove into her, the soft, silky lips of her sex closing tightly over him. "Sweet little thing."

She closed around him, wet and soft, an eager moan falling from her lips as he lowered his head to catch a nipple between his teeth. He surged inside, gripping her soft, rounded ass and grinning when she squealed as he pushed his finger against her anus.

Aryn held back until he felt the orgasm start to ripple through her, and then he rammed into her repeatedly, until the climax broke free.

He then took her to the bed and guided her head down until she could wrap her pretty little lips around his cock, groaning with delight and she set to the task with obvious, unfaked pleasure. Her round, firm ass stayed high in the air as she worked him, and Aryn's hand closed around one soft white globe, massaging the flesh while his other hand wrapped in her loose hair. Occasionally, because that pretty butt just seemed to want it, he would give it a sharp little smack with the flat of his hand.

Her soft curls tossed over her shoulder, she stared at him through her lashes. Pulling away and swabbing the head of his penis with her tongue she then moved down to suckle and nibble on his sac before taking him into her mouth again. Moving slowly down the thick, rounded head, she took as much of him into her mouth as she could, falling into a slow steady rhythm that soon had Aryn lifting his hips to her caress and moaning.

The ruddy flesh of his cock gleamed wet as it slid in and out of her mouth, her hand gripping the base of his shaft, holding it steady as she moved. She slid the other hand under his hip, gripping a firmly muscled buttock and massaging.

"Oh, that was tasty," she murmured after he came in her mouth. Swallowing it down, licking her lips, she stroked his penis lovingly as she sat down next to him. "Should I be goin' now, sirrah?"

"Hell, no." Her eyes widened in surprise when she felt his very hard penis start probing the entrance to her vagina.

Aryn thought later that the little servant had been the answer to a prayer. He spent the night ridding himself of the desperate need to ride a woman and come inside her warm body. And she was tempting. Tempting enough, pretty enough, he almost gave in to the silent question in her eyes before he ushered her out of the room.

But, no, he wasn't letting her stay, wasn't buying her contract, wasn't going to wake up and ride her one last time before he headed out. As much as he wanted to.

As he drifted off to sleep a little later, he wondered one last time about the pretty, wild-eyed elf he had seen.

* * * * *

The pretty wild-eyed elf had paid for the room and rid it of its vermin. The bed was lumpy but she'd slept on worse. The room was warm enough since she had chosen the one right over the kitchen.

And she had been serenaded by the sound of various couples fucking.

It wasn't that she was jealous. Exactly. But the man wouldn't have had to pay a whore. Tyriel would have been more than happy to join him in bed that night.

Grumbling to herself, she settled down, clapping her pillow over her head to drown out the noise of lovemaking and sex play. Damnation, she wanted some play herself. The breathy moans coming from two doors down were driving her mad. Her incredibly sharp hearing could pick up the sounds and whispered orders as if she were in the room.

Her body was tight and aching and her nipples were beaded, pressing against her soft cotton shift. With an oath, she tore the shift off, her careless jerks rending it to shreds. Her hand crept down between her thighs and she closed her eyes, listening as Aryn told the servant to spread her legs. Tyriel's opened and she sought and found the hard little nub just atop her wet slit.

Her hand moved in fast little circles, desperate for some release of the pressure inside her belly.

Too long. She had been alone far too long.

A sobbing moan left her lips, agony coursing through her. Not enough. Not enough. Frustrated need and magick coursed through her blood, conjuring a phantom out of thin air. The phantom was nothing more than an illusion, a very touchable illusion that, thanks to Tyriel's mindless need, had a large cock that slid against her cleft as a mouth came crashing down on hers, obeying her every silent wish. That hot, avid mouth settled on her nipple, first one then the other, suckling gently, then hungrily until she had reached up and gripped handfuls of silky hair.

Strong hot hands moved over her body, gripping her hips, stroking her along the sensitive crease between her buttocks as the phantom spread her thighs and plunged inside her aching cleft with one deep, surging thrust that stole her breath, riding her headlong into climax, granting her release before fading back into nothingness.

When Tyriel could finally, finally, breathe around the need that had been plaguing her for weeks, starting to suffocate her for the past few days, she rolled over into her pillow and slept.

And down the hall, the mattress continued to thrum and squeak. She roused briefly, mumbled under her breath, magick whispered through the room, then blissful quiet fell over her as the shield of silence fell.

Tyriel woke early.

There was one last thing she had to do.

And she was leaving, even if she didn't have as much money saved as she had planned.

* * * * *

"Of all the damned fools," Tyriel hissed as she faced down the guard who stood at the gate, attempting to bar her way out of the city.

"Taxation for leaving the city?" she replied icily, one black brow rising expectantly as the guard continued to hold out one grimy hand.

How had this towne slid so far downhill in the few short years since she had visited last? Mentally, she counted back and was somewhat disconcerted to realize it had been nearly fifteen years, not the two or three she had thought at first. Sighing, she shoved her hair back. When you were alone, time had a way of slipping by with little notice.

"I was taxed when I entered, when I contracted a short job acting as bodyguard, when I paid for my room and board, and whenever I made a purchase. And you expect me to pay more simply for leaving?"

"Pay your dues, milady," the guard repeated. "O'course, iffen yer short money, we kin work it out." His eyes landed on her mouth, letting her know exactly how she could work it out.

I'd rather bite it off than suck it, nasty little man.

"No. No, I don't think so," she said slowly, after appearing to ponder the matter. "Perhaps I'll go make my complaints known to the constable and have him explain this new tax to me. And I can ask how exactly I am expected to pay it off. Then, perhaps I'll pay." She turned and studied the street behind her, frowning thoughtfully. "I believe his office is at the towne center, just to the right of the rather gaudy and filthy fountain. Is that right?"

The slight widening of the guard's eyes answered her question. There was no taxation. But few people thought to question it, she supposed. Even fewer made mention of the constable. The damned guards in this towne grew worse every trip.

Of course, there had been a time when this had been a decent city, with good decent folk, honest servants. No slaves.

And no indiscriminate screwing on street corners.

"What? No response?" she asked dryly as the guard's hand fell and he glared at her sullenly. "I'll just take my leave then."

With a smile, she led her horse through the gate and off the road, pausing just long enough to check the riding gear and her own supplies. Then she swung up on the horse and offered a cheery wave before nudging Kilidare onto the road.

Her nearly empty coin purse slapped against her hip as the horse took off at a ground-eating gallop. Good thing he hadn't decided to press the issue. Tyriel doubted she would have bothered with going to the constable and this morning's purchase had near emptied her resources, for the time. Of course, she could always change that. Da would be more than happy, even rather insistent on changing that.

And she was rather insistent that he not.

She had made it by on far less than she had now. She could do it again.

* * * * *

"Sold?" Aryn repeated, staring at the barkeep with shuttered eyes. By the Holy Fire, he thought angrily. One of the patrons that had kept shooting the boy looks. Pretty child slaves didn't last long in places like this. They usually ended up in private homes or whorehouses. How could such filth be legal? Why was it allowed? His gut roiled and his hand ached for his sword.

He would find him.

That was all there was to it.

Shifting the harness at his shoulders, he closed his eyes. A headache was starting to pound behind his eyes, a familiar one. The blade at his back had that odd heavy feel to it. West, they had to ride west, find the child…soon, nay, not soon, now.

He shook his head as the odd spell of dizziness swarmed up. Shoving it back, Aryn clenched his hands and focused. The boy. He had to focus on the boy. Damn it! If he had seen to it last night instead of having his cock ridden — ah, but it was too late now.

No. He'd seen what was done to too many of the slave children.

If he could help just one —

Aryn had no idea what he would do with a small child while he traveled, but he would come up with something.

With eyes as cold and hard as winter ice, he looked back at the barkeep. He drew the long-bladed knife he wore at his hip and started to stroke the edge of it absently as he asked in a soft, silky purr, "To whom?"

The barkeep's eyes widened as the menace started to flow from one who had been fairly easy-going. He had stayed out of trouble, hadn't touched any of the wenches, save for the indentured one, and she had been fair glowing this morn. Hadn't complained about the food or the ale and now, over one boy, he was drawing a wicked looking knife. He licked his dry lips and replied, "The little elf las' night that saved 'is lazy arse up and paid for 'im afore headin' out this mornin'."

A smile spread across his face and the relief he felt was unreal. "Any idea where she was heading?" Aryn asked, wondering why he wasn't surprised.

The smile had the tension inside the barkeep's chest loosening, turning to greed. "Mebbe."

Aryn turned the knife, letting it catch the dull light as he cocked his head and studied the barkeep. He arched a brow, waiting. "Maybe?" he repeated. When no answer came, he slammed the knifepoint into the bar, reached out, snagged the barkeep's filthy shirt and dragged him up until they were nose to nose. "I suggest you remember, and remember fast. Else you are going to have a difficult time running this sorry inn—because I am going to cut out your tongue and shove it down your throat. And if I'm still feeling...edgy, I'll chop off your dick as well."

Rapidly, the barkeep said, "M' boy saw 'er loadin' the boy up w' the caravan that was outside t' wall las' night. Right happy, the boy looked." His face was pale, save for two spots of color high on his cheeks. "The gypsies have him now. And I didna lay a hand on t' boy. Gave 'er a good price, I did."

"There is no good price on a life," Aryn said in disgust, dropping him abruptly and shoving him back. "Perhaps I should take your boy and let the gypsies have him as well. And you could buy him back, for a price. But then, he would know true happiness, and he would never want to leave them for you."

He left, grabbing his pack and hitting the streets. His contract to the wagon train was up and he was free. If he didn't get away from this blasted city, he would go mad.

Chapter Two

"Eh, thas jes' a bloody girl."

Hmm. He is a bright one, isn't he? Tyriel thought with some amusement as the man in question stood several feet away from her, scratching his head and eyeing her dubiously.

"Ye takin' to bringing whores along?" the dunce asked, too stupid to recognize the warning in his boss's eyes and the fire in Tyriel's.

But she kept her voice mild as she said, "I'm not here to whore for anybody."

"I've not seen many her equal when it comes to a sword," Gerome said with a glare. "If she can keep my wagons safe, that's all that matters to me."

Crossing his arms over his massive chest, the surly fellow eyed Tyriel with derisive eyes. "I ain't workin' alongside no bloody girl," he said confidently, certain Tyriel would be sent packing. "Unless'n I kin be putting her under me."

Gerome eyed the fellow with pursed lips, then shrugged his shoulders. "All right. Aldy, get Benjin's wages together. He gave me three days of work."

"Huh?"

Aldy, the tiny, spry little man who had hired Tyriel in towne the past night, scurried over to the hulking idiot who stood staring at Gerome as if he had grown a second head.

"Wages? I thought we didn't get paid 'til the trip was done." The dunce reached up to scratch his straw-colored hair a second time.

"The trip is done for you. You won't work beside a girl and I have no intention of passing by an excellent swordsman and mage in favor of you," Gerome said, dismissing Benjin by introducing Tyriel to the cook and two other guards.

"There's Aryn," Gerome said, pointing off in the distance to a figure on horseback.

When Tyriel glanced back at Benjin one last time, the man still stood there, scratching his head and looking puzzled.

* * * * *

"You."

Tyriel raised her head, one hand holding a suede cloth, stroking it up and down the length of her blade.

The man in front of her stood with his back to the sun, towering over her. Raising one hand to shield her eyes, Tyriel made out the features of the swordsman from the inn she had met the previous fall. "Yes, me," she replied evenly.

"I wondered if the Tyriel Gerome told me about was the one I had met a few months back."

"Looks like it," she said cheerfully, sliding her blade into its sheath. "Aryn, is it?"

"I didn't know the kin hired themselves out to wagon trains," Aryn said, squatting down beside her. Damp tendrils of hair clung to the sides of his face and neck and his bared chest glistened with sweat. And it was every bit as fine as she had imagined it would be, wide, sculpted, muscled. His arms were roped with muscle, but not overly so, his shoulders wide and powerful, and she imagined, just perfect for resting your head on.

After.

Oh, yummy.

Hmmm. Maybe, just maybe, this trip could turn out to be rather pleasant. Very pleasant. If he would just...cooperate.

Since the day was rather cool, Tyriel guessed he had been practicing. Nodding at the shallow nick on his forearm, she asked, "That happen in practice?"

Glancing at it, dismissing it, Aryn said, "Yes. The short, stocky guy with a beard and no hair, Dule. He's got a fast hand. How did you end up hiring your blade out? I've never known a lady of the elves to want to leave the wonder of their lands for ours."

"I'm a breed, Aryn," she said shortly, sliding into her harness and rising to her feet. "You know what that means? I don't belong with the kin. And as much as I love my mother's folk, I can only take so much of them at a time."

"Who are your mother's folk?"

One slim black brow rose into the air. "You're not as closemouthed as I would have expected," she mused, shaking her head. And then she reached up, grabbing a hand full of springy black curls. "With hair like this, who else? The gypsies, of course."

A laugh tumbled from Aryn's unbelievably beautiful mouth as he went from kneeling beside her to lying flat on his back, knees drawn up. Staring up at the blue sky, he continued to laugh, his chest shaking, his eyes crinkling up and sparkling with mirth. "Oh, bloody hell. That is rich. The gypsy lady and a lord of the kin—I'd think an angel and an incubus would have made a better match."

"Quite possibly." A sad, bittersweet smile tugged at her lips and her exotic eyes took on a faraway look. "But we'll never know. My mother died in childbirth. If she hadn't been with the kin when she went into labor, I wouldn't be here." Shrugging her slim shoulders, she said, "I can say, without hesitation, I had an interesting childhood."

"Who raised you?" He slowly sat up, still grinning.

Dusting her hands off, she rose to her feet, eyeing the swordsman with pursed lips and narrowed eyes. Her topaz eyes flashed and glowed and Tyriel felt raw emotion swirling inside her and threatening to spill out. The air around them thickened as though a storm threatened.

Tyriel could see his eyes widen in acknowledgment and saw the darkening caused by nerves in the almost dreamy blue of his eyes. She heard the skipping of his heart caused by something akin to fear as her uncontrolled emotions caused power to pump from her in waves.

Then she swallowed it down, blinked and turned on her heel, walking away from him.

Who raised you?

Lowering her eyes to the stream that flowed around her bare feet, Tyriel wondered why the question had upset her so much. She had loved her father, still did, and knew that he loved her. Keeping her isolated from her mother's family had been a misguided attempt to protect her. And Da was a good father, had always been kind, loving, generous—most unelflike. At least to a half-breed.

The High Prince of Eivisa had spoiled her bloody rotten, and many still felt he should have sent her to the gypsies, or to an elvish brothel. Not that they would dare say that to their Prince's face, or his daughter's.

With a sigh, she acknowledged that he had done what he had thought was best, what he had thought was right. Keeping her isolated from all—the kin and the gypsies—trying to protect the mongrel child from the slights of being of mixed race.

He couldn't have known, or understood, how easily and deeply the gypsies gave their love. Not when the elves rarely gave anything easily, and loved nothing deeply, save themselves and their own. Oh, they loved a lost cause, the poor, the broken down and the pitiful. But Tyriel was anything but—she had an elf's pride, a Princess' arrogance, and the magick of two powerful races flowing through her veins.

Perhaps if she had been a foundling, or an abused child one of the kin had saved, they would have loved and cherished her. Rather odd that the Prince had fathered her, and for that they had rejected and despised her. They should have loved her more. If he hadn't spent the last seventy years mourning her mama, if he had taken a bride from their people, an elvish bride, maybe, just maybe, they wouldn't have held such a grudge.

But a gypsy lover was unlike anything they could fathom, Tyriel thought with a small smile.

Just the love a gypsy gave was incomparable, but to have a gypsy lover—her heart kicked up a notch as she remembered her first gypsy lover, a wild gypsy youth, who was now a chieftain, and a grandfather.

When she had arrived among them some forty years earlier, she had been welcomed with open arms and happy hearts. And by the men with hot eyes and bold smiles…ah, the memories! Everything the gypsies did, they did with passion and life—it was no wonder her father had no desire to seek a new bride among the kin.

The elves—they were seduction and magick, lovely magick, yes. But sometimes that magick was so very painful. And that was why he had kept her alone, away from the kin.

But the gypsies were passion and fire, and everything wonderful.

Keeping her isolated from the kin had been to protect her. That intention had been well-thought out.

It wasn't his fault she had gone against his wishes and gone out among the kin where she had learned just how very cruel her father's people could be. How very arrogant.

How very…elvin.

Absently, she fingered the elongated curve of her ear, so much longer than that of her human kin, yet not pointed enough for many of the elves to accept her.

Rejection was something she had never experienced, until the summer of her eighteenth birthday. By the Blood, she had been so happy, so excited, at the thought of learning about her people. She had planned the escape from her protective papa for nearly two months, slipping out during her birthday celebration. Within her father's lands, his keep alone, she was protected, coddled, adored...his people loved and worshipped her. The few that might have made slights against her...well, there may well have been some, but they never made it known to her.

She was well-protected, well-shielded against reality.

Perhaps too well. Had she been exposed to some true elvish ways, perhaps she wouldn't have been so eager to go out into the realm alone, without her father or his men at her side.

But Tyriel had so badly wanted to learn more about what was beyond the walls of her father's keep, exotic though it was. Wanted to know more about the kin than what her father had revealed.

A long wonderful night of revelry, dancing and laughing with a handsome lord who smiled and whispered so seductively to her, leading her to a room as he used elvish magick to blind her eyes to the men who followed, the ones who would block her magick and her attempts to escape. Eighteen was young for an elf, way too young for her to battle off an attack—and that was what came, as they jeeringly jerked the cover from her eyes, told her she was good for nothing but whoring for her betters, that she was a misfit who should have died at birth, would have died at birth if her father had been anybody less than who he was — while they pinned her to a wall and tore away the pretty gown she had been given for her birthday ball.

They didn't realize though that the half-breed had more than elvish magick. As she screamed in fury, her body went red hot and pulsed. One fell back, shrieking in pain as she lashed out and struck him, leaving a burned mark on him — touch of fire, gypsy magick — her hand on his throat, unable to let go until it had burned completely through and he gasped out his last breath as Tyriel sent up a cry that tore down the barriers they had put up. Her father's attempts to isolate her had worked quite well. Not only did she know little about the elvish world, the kin knew too little about her and how strong she was.

Prince Josah, the High Prince of Eivisa, had already been out searching for her, his body tight with rage and fury as he sensed her fear through their link, but was unable to track her. When the barrier shattered, he homed in on her like a beacon, his dark assassin, Jaren following silently in his wake.

It was Jaren who took off his cloak and covered the nearly nude Princess, leaving the four living elvish lords to his Prince, unable to deny him that satisfaction, though by rights he should have taken their lives before risking his Prince. But he judged by the blood in the Prince's eyes, none would live more than a few heartbeats.

Tyriel closed her eyes, shaking her head as the memories swarmed up so strongly. Her father had struck like an avenging angel — striking the men down before they realized what had happened. She had killed the first one and then cowered in the corner as they milled around her, trying to figure out how to dispose of her without touching her, staring at the fallen body of their friend.

You should have died...

And some Royals would have let her. Some elves may have refused to deliver a half-breed's child.

But when a Prince of the people said "Save my child," the kin damn well knew that to fail was to mark their own doom.

Tyriel had found her place in Averne, the elvish realms, after spending a decade training in the Hall of Warriors. Tyriel wasn't truly an elvish assassin, but she was a warrior, and none would dare look down their aristocratic noses at her behind her father's royal back ever again. She could slit their throats while they drank their wine and they would never know it until they fell down dead.

And her father would stand by and applaud. Eivisa was the largest and most powerful of the elvish realms of Averne, and none dared to challenge him. And many, though none dared to voice it, felt shame for what had nearly happened to her.

It could be seen in their eyes when she walked by. She bore the mark of an elvish princess in her carriage, in her gaze, written all over her long graceful body.

And her father's love and pride in her shone from him every time he looked at her or spoke of her.

Loving his wild gypsy wife had changed something inside him.

Losing her had changed it even more.

But Tyriel—she made the biggest difference.

"I miss you, Da," she whispered, reaching up to stroke the amber-colored moonstone beneath her jerkin. It lay side by side with another chain, this one from the gypsies, a crucifix, a symbol of the Sacrificed God, lost so long ago, only the gypsies and the Kin still remembered His Name, and few but the gypsies still worshipped Him.

An odd heat answered her and she smiled. Somewhat less melancholy, she lay back on the bank to enjoy the fading sun.

She smirked a little.

How would the elves feel if they knew that the gypsies they so looked down upon were one of the only remaining races that still believed in the One God they also believed in?

Chapter Three

When she came back to camp later that night—much later—Aryn shifted on his bedroll to watch her glide through the sleeping bodies on the ground. She was unbelievably quiet, gliding on feet so silent she didn't even disturb the animals sleeping throughout the camp.

She paused a few feet away, and though Aryn could barely make out her form, much less her face, he knew she was watching him, that she could see him clear as day. He didn't have to see her to recall that form, those wild black curls, her large slanted eyes, winged black brows, a red kissable mouth and that tiny mole right by her lips.

Tall, reed-slender, small-breasted and slim-hipped— she shouldn't have been quite so enticing, he knew. But every damn time she bent over, he saw the tight, rounded ass and wanted to grasp her hips and drive into her, see how tight and snug her sheath was, how wet she was, what she tasted like.

He burned...to know if the fire he saw in her eyes, sensed beneath her skin was as real as he suspected it was. Ached, so badly his cock throbbed every time he caught a breath of her intoxicating scent.

Her eyes were starting to haunt him at night, and her low, husky laugh, the way her magick seemed to shimmer in the air around her. But it was more than that. She had something that drew words from him, something that made him open up. And Aryn was rarely open.

What was it about her? he wondered as she continued on past him without speaking. He was closemouthed, or had always thought himself to be, until just a few marks earlier. How had she frozen him in place with simply a look? Why was it his flesh prickled every time she was near?

Not his cock. That did not prickle—it stiffened, hardened and ached.

With a sigh, Aryn flipped onto his back, flung his arm over his eyes and ordered himself to sleep.

God above knew, sunrise came awful early to a mercenary.

Though she had slid into her bedroll far later than the others, Tyriel was the first to rise, stretching her arms high overhead before bending over to touch her toes, loosening muscles stiffened from a night on the cold ground. Rolling her head on her shoulders, she eyed the sleeping camp.

Rain was coming. The damp, earthy scent was faint on the wind and the rain probably wouldn't hit until later in the day; with hope, it would even hold off until they made camp tonight.

Grabbing her pack, she headed to the stream for some privacy before the others woke.

A short time later, Tyriel wound her wet hair into a braid and flipped the long tail over her shoulder. Stuffing her clothes and soap into the pack, Tyriel rose with a smile and an appreciative sniff. The cook was up and had cava going.

The thick, rich scent of it had her mouth watering and she was almost able to ignore the heavy, greasy scent of bacon. Poor little pig, she thought sympathetically as she made her way back to camp.

But that was the way of it. And even if the thought of eating meat turned her stomach, it didn't bother her if the humans ate it, providing it didn't come in contact with her own food.

Few people, very few people, outside the kin knew that meat was akin to poison to an elf. The proteins found in meat were far too strong for an elf's system and if ingested in large enough amounts, it could cause the body to fail. The heart couldn't beat right, the blood thickened as the reaction strengthened, and eventually, if not treated, the elf could die.

Which was why so few people knew.

With such a strong weakness, if their enemies knew —

The enemies of the kin were many, coveting their wealth, coveting their mines, coveting the magick that flowed so easily from one generation to the next.

"Good morning."

Turning her head, she smiled at Aryn as he stepped from the trees, a pack like her own hanging limply from one hand. "I'm done. It's all yours."

"I believe that. I doubt the majority of our fellow campers have ever heard of the concept of regular bathing," Aryn said wryly.

Remembering the oily stench of unwashed bodies, Tyriel adopted a horrified expression. "Bathe? As in regularly? But baths cause the pneumonia," she squealed, fluttering her hands in the air.

"I've heard that." A wide grin lit his lean face. "I guess I'll just have to take my chances."

Waving to the stream with a broad gesture, Tyriel offered, "Go ahead. Dunk yourself—commit suicide. I'll tuck the blankets around you when the pneumonia has its hold on you."

"How kind." His eyes lingered briefly on the damp tunic that clung to her before he turned away.

The hesitation was enough. Her highly attuned senses could pick up the sound of his heart when it sped up a tiny bit, the scent that spilled out of his pores when he was aroused.

Tyriel was proud to admit she was only slightly tempted to linger in the trees and spy on the blond swordsman as he washed up. Just a little tempted.

As she turned, her eyes landed on the sword he took off. Still in its sheath, it leaned up against a nearby stone, within easy reach. Even as she turned to walk down the path, it seemed to draw her eyes again. The runes and marking on the hilt were...familiar.

And for some reason that temptation was even stronger than the one to play voyeur while Aryn bathed.

If honor didn't run so strong in her blood, Tyriel just might have tried to take the blade, just for a bit.

The blade seemed to be calling her.

New moon.

Lying on the ground, listening to the silence, Tyriel studied the star-spangled sky overhead. Near the western horizon, a dark circle hung in the air, where the moon would be in a few more nights.

The air had a heavy feel to it. Almost sticky. Very odd, considering how cool the night air was. Rolling on her side, she stared into the fire, hardly even aware that she drifted into sleep.

When she awoke a short time later, the camp had grown quiet, abnormally so. Even the breathing of the mercenaries around her seemed quieter than normal. Closing her eyes, she slowed her own breathing and reached out with her senses. Even the heartbeats seemed to be slowed. Dropping her shielding, she let her sense of self flow into the ground beneath her and she shrank back from what she found — tampering with the life force, the ebb and flow of the magick in the earth, in the people.

There was mischief and magick afoot. Bad magick. Slowly, she looked around before she sat up. They were all sound asleep. Unbelievably sound.

Rising, Tyriel took her sword in hand and slid it out of its sheath. Turning in a circle, she studied the camp, counted bodies. All were accounted for.

Her ears pricked and she turned, cocking her head, staring into the woods that lay just to the east of their camp. A threat. Her own heartbeat kicked up and her breathing became softer, shallower as she struggled to pin down what had alerted her instincts.

Her eyes were drawn to the woods and the warrior inside her whispered that this was where the threat lay hidden. But the other half of her, the guardian, commanded she stay.

Slowly, she lowered herself to the ground, her long legs folding beneath her. She put her back to the fire, lay her blade across her lap, and stared into the woods.

The threat, whatever it was, would go through her first.

As it was, it was a very long night. The first of many.

* * * * *

"I tell you, I'll do nothing as long as she is within the camp," the first voice repeated.

"A deal was made," a second, weaker, rasping voice refuted. "You'll abide by it, or else."

"When the deal was made, there was no elvin kin within the camp. If you think I'll take on the likes of her, you are sorely mistaken."

A growl rumbled from the other's throat. "What if she isn't within the camp? Can you do it then?"

Head tilted to the side, the first pursed his lips and pondered. "If given enough time, I can do it."

"Then do it. I must have it."

"And the mercenary?"

Skinny shoulders rose and fell in a disinterested shrug. "Whatever is easiest for you."

The sleepless nights were beginning to take their toll. Even though the kin required minimal sleep, they did require some recharging. And it had been nearly three weeks since Tyriel had gotten a good night's sleep. Every time she drifted close to sleep, somebody woke her, purposely or by accident.

And the feeling of being watched never lessened. Tyriel had taken to wearing a crucifix around her neck, acknowledging the superstitions of her mother's people. The Sacrificed God would no doubt snicker at the thought of saving one such as her, but from time to time, she was able to rest, one hand curled around it.

"You're not looking well, Tyriel."

Looking up, she met the gaze of the healer contracted to ride with the caravan. Clad in robes of gray, signifying his school in the gray arts, Mitchan stood watching her with concern on his bony face.

"I'm fine, Healer." With deliberate care, Tyriel slid the stone up and down the length of her blade.

"You don't seem to sleep very well," he noted, eyeing the circles under her golden eyes. "Perhaps I could offer you a tonic?"

"Most of the tonics made for humans are either worthless on my kind, or deadly. But thank you for offering," she said, concentrating on her sword.

"I've studied with the elvin kin. I know some of the remedies used by them. I've some moonwart and polyseed."

Simple herbal sleep remedies, very commonly used among the kin. Studying the nondescript brown eyes of the healer, Tyriel pegged him as an honest enough man, even if his art was something that didn't appeal to her.

Gray-robed or not, he did know his healing, she knew. She'd kept an eye on him from day one, leery of the line he walked that was sometimes so close to the blacker arts.

But—call her paranoid—she wasn't accepting anything more than a cup of water from Mitchan, or anybody else on this train. She trusted very few, and he certainly was not on the list.

"Thanks, Healer. But I will be fine."

It was late that morning, just before the midday break when she acknowledged that she was not fine. Lack of sleep was starting to make her slightly ill. Clambering into the wagon, she shot Dule a grateful glance. "Just a nap and I'll be well."

Of the sixty-odd members of the caravan, Tyriel trusted only three. Dule, who was as honest as the day was long, Aryn, with those sinful eyes and Gerome, who was too damn greedy to do a damn thing that would endanger his caravan.

Of those three, Dule was the only one she felt safe in confiding her exhaustion.

Not that it had taken her confiding in him. He had been watching her for a couple of days and just a short while ago had ordered her to rest that day. She dropped to the small cot inside the wagon, stretched on her belly, folded her hands under her head, and was asleep in less than a heartbeat.

"Have you seen Tyriel?"

Dule glanced down at the blond swordsman who had guided his horse to the side of the wagon. A scowl twisted his mouth as he shifted; recalling the blow the boy had delivered during their last practice.

"She's resting."

"Resting?" Aryn repeated, his brows rising. "In the middle of the day?"

"She's exhausted. So I told her to rest."

"Why is she exhausted?"

"I didn't ask. I assume something is bothering her and keeping her from resting well at night."

A new voice called Dule's name in the distance. Through the dust, he could make out the Healer's gray robe. Sliding Aryn a glance, he said, "Quiet, now."

"I was wondering, have you seen Tyriel?" Mitchan asked. "I've been trying to watch her for the past few days. She doesn't look well."

"She's off doing an errand for me," Dule lied. "She'll catch up with us later."

Bushy black brows rising, Mitchan asked, "But isn't that her horse tied behind your wagon?"

"I sent her on mine. Her horse picked up a rock last night. He doesn't need to do any heavy work for a day or two."

Aryn frowned, turning his head away while Mitchan talked with Dule a few more moments. Keeping his voice low, Aryn asked after Mitchan rode away, "What is going on? Why didn't you tell him she is sleeping?"

"Do me a favor, run and set me horse loose for a bit—whack his flank and tell him to get feed. He knows what that means, and he'll come back when he's through. Be quick, and be back fast. Don't let that healer see you, either, else I'll slice your pretty face up," Dule said sharply, keeping an eye on Mitchan's back as he headed for the front of the train.

Aryn frowned and opened his mouth to snap back but Dule said, "For the lass, boy?"

Aryn's brows lowered and he sighed, guiding his horse around and galloping to the back of the train, relying on instinct and his gut, but double-checking, just to be sure, that Mitchan had not followed. Bloody weapons master had best be quick to offer an explanation, he groused as he smacked the horse's flank. The ugly beast took off eagerly, his intelligent eyes wide and bright as he clambered up the hill that bordered the side of the trail, nimble-footed as a mountain goat.

"I don't trust him." Dule didn't even wait for Aryn to demand an explanation when he returned, just opened his mouth and baldly stated those four words.

"He's a healer. If you can't trust him, who can you trust?"

"Myself," Duel replied with a sneer. "He's a gray Healer, so any covenants he made when he took on his robes are subject to his own approval. He may not violate the laws of nature when he heals, but he doesn't have a problem violating the laws of man."

Casting a worried glance to the back, Dule said, "And it ain't jes that she's not sleepin'. Ain't been doin' that fer a while now. And now, she up and naps in the middle of the day. Somethin's up."

Aryn had been around too many times not to feel his skin prickle when Dule said that. "We've got problems coming?" he asked mildly as the blade at his back became noticeably heavier, and started to pulse. Odd—it seemed like it had done this before. And then an odd, muffled feeling pushed at his mind and he forgot that thought.

"Dunno. She be the one to ask." Sliding Aryn a glance, he said, "Somethin' 'bout the fae that jes' plain bothers me. When they start acting all twitchy-like, you know somethin's up. And hell, half the time, I dunno if I wanna know."

With a laugh, Aryn said, "I know what you mean, old man."

With a sigh, Dule reached up and scratched his bald head. It was bald by his own hand, not by God's. Daily, he scraped it smooth with the edge of the wicked knife he carried at his side. "Nope. I don' wanna know. We jes deal with it when it's here."

Chapter Four

Tyriel awoke feeling sluggish.

Bracing her hands under her, she pushed up from the small mat Dule slept on. Thank God the man was clean, she thought hazily as she looked around.

My head, she thought. Reaching for it, she cradled it between her hands and concentrated, trying to clear the haze. How long had she slept?

That was when she realized night had fallen.

Cocking her head, she peered through the small opening in the rear of the wagon.

It couldn't be that late.

Not a soul was moving.

Dule had promised to wake her before they stopped for the night.

Silently, she rose, blinking her eyes rapidly and taking slow, deep breaths. As she breathed, the cobwebs cleared from her mind much slower than they should have.

Sliding from the wagon, Tyriel peered around.

They hadn't stopped for the night. It was as if they had just stopped for the afternoon watering and not moved since. Unable to move.

Creeping around to the front of the wagon, Tyriel peered into the still frozen face of Dule.

For one horrible moment she thought he was dead.

Reaching out, she placed her fingers on his wrist, felt the slow pulse. Dangerously slow, especially for a human. His eyes were wide-open and frozen, his mouth open as if about to speak.

Hissing, Tyriel jerked her hand back.

Mind magick.

One hand moved in an age-old symbol of protection as she faded back into the shadows cast by the wagon. There was no moon and the night was eerily silent. No sounds of a camp settling down for the night, no birds calling, no horses snuffling in their feed.

Silently, Tyriel moved to the next wagon and stared into the face of another frozen man. The cook and his wife sat staring at each in other in a bizarre moment of affection they would never let the rest of the camp see.

Each wagon, each horse and rider showcased another frozen statue.

Only two were missing.

Mouth drawn back in a snarl, she searched the camp a second time, trying to find them. But they were not there.

Both Aryn the swordsman and Mitchan the Grey were missing.

Reaching up, she closed one hand around her crucifix and prayed a brief prayer.

And then she fell to her knees and drew a tiny knife from the belt at her waist.

First, she carved a circle in the earth.

Then she spat into it. With the knife, she cut the tip of her left index finger and smeared her blood into the saliva and dirt.

Rearing up, she held the knife high overhead, chanted under her breath and drove it into the earth. Enchantment—not one of her stronger gifts, but at times, it had its uses.

Moments later, the earth shifted and a small sphere rose from the circle she had drawn in the earth.

After murmured words from Tyriel, the sphere cleared...spinning, waiting.

Another whispered order and now it held three faces. Two she had never seen before, but she recognized them from the looks in their eyes, the cut of their clothes. Mercenaries.

Bandits would be a better word. Their type rarely worked the way a mercenary did, preferring to hide and attack and pilfer. The third, though, she knew.

Mitchan.

"Where?" she whispered, rising to her feet.

As she rose, the sphere drifted in an eastern direction. Toward the woods. To the west was the Shojurn River. The caravan followed the path that headed north, to Shojurn City, still nearly three weeks away. If she remembered correctly, and she was certain she did, the nearest village was three days away and not even equipped with a militia.

But where was Aryn?

The globe went blank, saying Aryn wasn't anywhere that her power could locate.

So, like Tyriel herself, Aryn was shielded.

Tyriel gestured fluidly to the camp and murmured, *"Ay vern noi." I cannot see you.* She murmured quietly in ancient elvish, "May the darkness protect and hold you." And as simple as that, the camp was gone—or so it seemed.

Illusion. A simple shield, but the sleeping people in the camp weren't the ones in danger.

Prowling through the woods, sword in hand, Tyriel searched. Countless circles, countless deer trails. She had already spied where the others were, the ones who hunted for their prey, and dodged them easily as they also prowled the woods.

When a hand shot out just behind her, Tyriel didn't hear or see anything until a blade was pressed to her throat, held by a very knowledgeable hand, with the sharp edge just to the right, where the large vessels lay. A bit different on an elf, but eh, she could still bleed to death if he cut deep enough.

She started to murmur under her breath, lifting one arm to plow back behind her when he spoke. A deep guttural voice, but his none the less.

"Hmm, ye are here t' cause harm but know—I'll go to none but the one who already bears me." The voice was Aryn's but the cadence, the rhythm, was not.

A wild and erratic primitive magick filled the air, swirling around her, blowing her hair back from her face, sending a prickle along her skin that told her what she had already suspected. Aryn's blade was enchanted. And there was something else—the magick that was in the sword was starting to settle inside him. He was no trueborn mage, but in time, he would be a mage, or enchanter, all the same.

"I mean no harm to him or the others. Only the ones who cast the sleep spell," she said slowly, lowering her sword and dropping her shields with a small fluid gesture of her hand.

"*Elf?*" he replied, in that same guttural voice. The hand around her throat started to urge her back, back against his body, until she was flush against him. His other hand stroked the moonstone at her neck, then stroking the crucifix that lay next to it as the moonstone glowed in recognition at his touch—how odd—and then he stroked the curve of her ears, though that wasn't how he knew her.

"Aye."

"Hmmm. Not just elf. Blood of my kin as well. Jiupsu," the deep guttural voice said, one hand stroking over her dense black curls. His other hand went from her throat to trail down the center of her chest, down her torso to spread flat over her belly. The knife was suddenly just gone as his hand spread wide open over her stomach, pressing flat and holding her flush against him. Against her back, she felt his cock swell and throb. "Jiupsu. The warriors who sing and dance—"

Jiupsu. Gypsy…the race we descended from, thousands of years ago, Tyriel thought, her head spinning. And she was wet, and aching, as a long, lingering throb went through her cleft. *What in the hell is going on?*

The unbelievably strong hand fell from her belly and she whirled around. And in those dark-blue eyes, she saw the shadow of something very ancient lurking. Possibly even more ancient than the history of the kin.

Conversationally, hands held up with palms out, she said, "I'd really like to know more about how you landed inside Aryn's body, but I think that needs to wait." Her eyes drifted to the east, deeper into the woods, and she said, "It's you they are searching for, isn't it?"

"Aye." A smile—a slow, sensual curl of his lips—formed and she had the disconcerting image of another man, taller, broader, with wind tossed curling black hair that fell to his waist, black gypsy's eyes, and a wicked, wicked smile...then sadness, deep and bitter.

"I doubted he was just looking for the sword. It's the power inside he seeks. To get that, he must forge a bond. With *you*." The being controlling Aryn turned, studying the direction Tyriel's eyes had gone. "And to get you, what will have to be done with Aryn?"

"My bearer must die before another can bond with me."

Blowing a breath out in a rapid whoosh, Tyriel said, "I was afraid you'd say that."

Those dark, familiar, yet unfamilar, eyes turned to her, puzzled. "Why? I willna let tha' happen. Ye willna either. And he's a powerful warrior. Why else would I have chosen him?"

Tyriel silently made a note. Ancient beings take things very literally. "No. I won't let that happen."

She shifted, slid her sword into its sheath and dropped to her haunches.

Cocking his head, Aryn/Ancient One studied her. "What are ye doing? No time to rest is this."

Peering up at him, she said, "I'm not resting." The blood on the tip of her finger had dried, and it was already tender, but again, she pierced it with her knife. "Elves are elemental mages. We draw our strength from the elements, we use the earth as our eyes, the wind as our ears, the trees and grasses can be our hands." One fat crimson drop of blood fell to the earth and soaked into the soil.

Staring into the earth, eyes squinted, Tyriel hummed under her breath. "Eight of them, nine if you count Mitchan the Grey. I hate to point out the obvious, but the healer wants his hands on you."

"No healer. Healing ability, perhaps. Knowledge of herbs, aye. But no healer. Are ye as...capable as Aryn thinks you are?"

"More." It was her turn to smile now.

They encountered two en route to the tiny camp Mitchan's bandits had set up. Tyriel had engaged in swordplay with the smaller one and completely missed what had happened to the second.

When she saw the gore staining Aryn's clothes, she decided it was better that way. The bloodlust she saw in those eyes was enough to make the skin on the back of her neck crawl. The power that hummed in the air between them had it all but crackling.

How does Aryn live with this being inside him? she wondered as she turned away. Pausing, she wiped the blood from her sword on the tunic of the fallen man, studiously avoiding what remained of his partner.

"Down to seven," she murmured.

* * * * *

"Where are they?" Mitchan growled, staring at the leader with smoldering eyes.

"I don't know," Elkir replied. "The elf wasn't gone as you said she was. The gods only know where she is lurking and nobody has been able to find the swordsman. Your spell didn't so much as touch him."

"Your paltry magick has done little good," Mitchan said. "Don't dare mock mine."

"If you'd used a bit o' yours, we mighta already found him," Elkir snapped, starting to turn away.

"A bit?" Mitchan replied silkily. One arched brow rose and his cold green eyes narrowed.

Elkir's legs were frozen to the ground. Unable to move, he looked up at Mitchan and said, "Let me go."

"A bit more, perhaps?"

An unseen hand closed around Elkir's groin, and twisted. The bandit paled, his eyes bulged.

"Watch your step, Elkir. And find that man," he snapped, flinging the bandit to the ground with a mere flex of his mind. "I will have that sword."

Crouched in the shadows, Tyriel glanced over at Aryn/Ancient One. *Why does he want you so badly?* she wondered. Tyriel had serious doubts that Mitchan could force a bond with the being. This creature had said he had *chosen* Aryn. Chosen. That had her believing that no bond could be made unless the being *wanted* it.

As men moved in the shadows, Tyriel forced her mind to the matter at hand. *I'll find out later*, she promised.

"Take the leader and three more," she signed in the trader's hand language. Hopefully, in addition to the other languages he had gleaned from Aryn's head, this being would understand it as well.

"And the gray," he signed back, gesturing with one hand over his head to indicate the healer's robe.

"I take the rest. Draw them out," she signed, tapping one hand to her chest. She beckoned for him to draw back with her. When they were some distance back, she deliberately snapped a stick in two with the heel of her boot.

As expected, two of the fighters were sent into the woods. The one Tyriel came upon was just a boy, really, the fear in his eyes touching her.

Enough that she left him tied to a tree, unconscious and certain to sleep until dawn. To insure his path didn't stay on this road, she left a glamour spell with him, and a whispered warning. "Continue this path and you'll die before you have your first woman."

When she came upon Aryn/Ancient One with his victim, Tyriel wished she had taken a bit more time. Both the kin and the gypsies tended to make their kills cleanly. She'd wager Aryn did too. When Aryn was in control.

But in ancient times, when this being actually was a living breathing...whatever he was, she imagined life was more savage, more brutal. And messy. Tyriel imagined if she were able to find any scrolls on the Jiupsu, she would learn they had been very creative and visceral warriors.

The eviscerated corpse slid to the ground while Tyriel turned away.

"Soft stomach?"

Tossing him a glance over her shoulder, she said, "Absolutely. That's more meat than I care to see in a month, much less one night."

Down to five.

After the third man sent out didn't come back, the four remaining gathered around the campfire with Mitchan shooting fulminating looks into the darkness.

Finally, he shouted, "Come out, Aryn of Olsted. Must you hide in the shadows like a coward?"

When the being next to her tensed, Tyriel reached out and clasped his arm. "Don't give him the satisfaction. We can take them, but not if we don't use our heads."

"He questions our honor. Our courage."

Tyriel wondered at the 'our' but sighed. Men thousands of years ago were essentially just like men now. Senseless. "He is baiting you, drawing you out to kill you — or rather Aryn — so he can take the sword and you. Is that how you want to prove your honor and courage?"

"Is this how the chieftain and your father raised you, Lady of the Jiupsu?" He loomed over her, his eyes narrowed and menacing, his body all but vibrating.

Tyriel cocked an eyebrow. "The chieftain is rather proud that I have a brain that I use. I'd bet he'd suggest you do the same. Let's think — not kill each other and the body you are wearing."

It took some convincing, but Tyriel was the one to leave the safety of the tree first, while her prehistoric counterpart made his way to the opposite side of the camp.

Tyriel simply sheathed her sword and walked out of the woods, well aware of the eyes that were drawn to her, one by one. When Mitchan turned and saw her, she smiled and waggled her fingers at him. "I decided I could use some of that moonwart."

She saw the thoughts flickering through his eyes. Lie or not? Play dumb or attack?

One corner of her mouth rose in a smirk, taunting him, and she guessed right. Mitchan decided on attack. Launching a volley of energy bursts at her, he shouted an order at the others.

Before they could work up the nerve to move on her, she glanced at the logs they sat on, the vines and weeds beneath and let her essence speak to the blood she had shed in the ground just moments before walking into the camp.

The sorcerer's first attack hadn't even died away and three of his men were cocooned in living webs of roots and vines.

"Give me a little credit," she said, shaking her finger at him. "The least you could have done was send that pathetic excuse of a mage after me."

With a blinding smile, Tyriel turned her glowing eyes on Elkir and said, "You should really go now."

Instead, Elkir rushed her.

Bracing herself, she leaped aside just as he got within grabbing distance. His hand closed around her ankle and they tumbled to the ground.

A muffled shriek came from Mitchan, but Tyriel was too busy fighting off the hulking brute who was trying to smash her head into the ground.

Wrenching one arm free, she smashed the flat of her hand into his nose and bucked when the pain blinded him. Rolling to her feet, she pulled a knife from the belt at her waist and used the hilt to knock him across the head.

She turned before he even hit the ground, but Mitchan already lay dead by the campfire, his neck snapped, twisted more than halfway around. Empty-eyed, he stared into the night as the one standing over him turned and studied Tyriel.

"He'd be wise to keep you as a friend, Elf," was all he said and then he was gone, disappearing into the woods faster than any human she had ever seen.

Chapter Five

Tyriel bided her time, made sure the other had left Aryn's body, and that she had her own wits about her before she approached Aryn nearly a week later.

His sword rested against a rock while he knelt beside the creek, splashing his face with cold water.

Dragging her eyes away from his bare chest, she reminded herself she was here about something serious, not to ogle his physique, fine as it was. But damn, it was so fine — sculpted, lean, muscled. Right now, water was trickling down it, dampening the waist of his drawstring trousers, a few drops of water on his knees as he completed his morning ablutions.

"Would you mind telling me about your sword?" she asked when he turned questioning eyes her way.

With a frown he said, "Not much to tell. It was left to me at my mentor's death. He'd gotten it from his. I've had it nearly twenty years now."

"Long time."

Aryn shrugged, drying his face on a coarse cloth before reaching up and securing his damp hair with a leather thong. The blue stone in his ear flashed and winked at her.

Twenty years of bearing that heavy piece of metal might have something to do with that chest, she mused. Mentally, she slapped herself, dragged her eyes away from his chest, focused on the extraordinary blue of his eyes.

"Did your mentor tell you much about it?"

"Other than where he'd gotten it, I don't think there was much to tell," Aryn said with a shrug. Reaching for his shirt, he tugged it over his head and tucked the ends of it inside his breeches before fastening a thick heavy leather belt around his waist.

The harness he slid into, shrugging his shoulders automatically until the weight of the sword was right. Then he focused his eyes on Tyriel, raised one golden brow and asked, "Why?"

Tyriel touched her lip with the tip of her tongue, studying him with shrewd eyes. He wasn't going to like what she had to say, but he would listen. And he'd believe. Even if he didn't want to. He had walked around, brooding, the day after the attack. He had known something was wrong, had sensed it, felt it. A few times she had sensed him questioning himself, then his eyes had gone dazed, and she had felt a rush of magick rise up.

The blade, the being inside it, was blocking him.

But part of him already suspected.

"May I?" she asked, holding out her hand.

Silently, Aryn reached behind him, drew the sword from its harness and handed it to her.

No wonder it had looked familiar. The words were a very, very ancient form of the old gypsy tongue — one that hadn't been spoken in probably two or three thousand years. Tracing one finger against the scrolled script, she whispered, "Irian." Raising her amber eyes to his, she said, "That means enchanter. This is very old."

"What else, little elf?" Aryn asked, his eyes dark and turbulent. In them, she saw a knowledge, something that was brewing and simmering. An awareness. And she also felt the awakening of the one inside him. The magick trying to rouse and cloud Aryn's mind. "I doubt its age means much to you."

"It wouldn't, except its age is part of what it is. Your sword is enchanted, Aryn. Or maybe I should say, possessed."

He was staring at her as if she had lost her mind. Tyriel sighed and stroked her brow. She most likely had. It was his fault—he was too bloody distracting. Long, lean, those broad shoulders, those deep blue eyes…ah, Tyriel, focus—focus! But it wasn't just the way he looked, or the way his fine butt filled out his breeches.

Something about him called to something inside of her, something she had never felt in all her years.

A smile tugged the corners of her mouth up and she handed the blade back to him. As she did, she made certain their hands touched, and she closed her other hand over his, focusing, whispering silently to the one inside his mind, as the clouds started to form in Aryn's mind. *I am telling him…he will know the truth… and know it today. Now go away.*

There it was…that first sign of surprise, and then disgruntlement. Then outright refusal. Tyriel whispered, silently, to that ancient thing alone, as she focused on Aryn, on his eyes, on his face, *I am not a mortal creature like the body you now inhabit, Jiupsu warrior. You try to enslave this man — I do not care for that at all.*

And now she felt his shock, then silence.

No, he had never seen it that way, had he?

"It hides itself very well. Maybe, though, I should say he hides himself very well. If something hadn't happened last week, I may not have known. He certainly doesn't want others knowing."

"He?" Aryn repeated, staring at the sword he held in his hand. Then he lifted his eyes to stare at her with suspicion. And resignation. Too many odd things had happened since he had first taken the blade, she suspected, for him not to realize there was truth to her words.

"Hmm. Definitely a 'he,'" Tyriel said. "He's taken your body over before, hasn't he?"

Those blue eyes darkened as Aryn stared at Tyriel, while she watched memories flicker through his eyes. Then his gaze became shuttered and he lowered his lashes until only a sliver of blue remained visible. He asked roughly, "What have I done?"

Tyriel's heart broke as she saw the horror in his dark eyes start to grow...she suspected he feared that he had done horrible things, and she could see him damning his body as he wondered if his own lusts had helped drive the Soul to do some wicked, awful crime against man. Gently, she said, "I don't think you've done anything wrong, anything you wouldn't have done of your own free will, if you had been given the choice. He was protecting you, and the camp, the night I realized what was going on. There's a warrior, a valiant one, residing inside the blade, make no mistake of that, Aryn. A man with a soul much like your own, I would imagine."

She relayed what she had awoken to that night a week earlier.

"So there wasn't something odd in the food. But I'd imagine you were the one who gave the cook the idea, aren't you?" Aryn asked, lowering himself to his heels and staring at the blade he held as if worried it might take on life and strike him dead.

"Yes. I...suggested it, rather strongly. I don't want the camp knowing..." her voice trailed off as she attempted to explain why she had concealed what had really happened.

"You don't want everybody knowing what you are," Aryn supplied, looking from the sword to her.

Meeting his eyes, Tyriel admitted, "Yes."

"Tell me what happened."

With a laugh, Tyriel lowered herself to the ground, her back propped against the rough trunk of the tree. "Believe it or not, it was Mitchan."

Sometime later, Tyriel stroked the side of Kilidare's neck, promising the bored elvish steed some excitement soon. What exactly, she didn't know. She'd conjure up some mock battle, if it would spare her the woebegone looks he kept giving her.

Not a pack horse, his sullen thoughts kept telling her.

"I know," she crooned, rubbing the strong neck beneath her hand.

"Frequently talk to yourself?"

Turning her head, she caught Aryn's amused eyes on her. "Yes, I do. But this time, I was talking to Kilidare," she told him, nodding at the stallion. The gray ears flickered and he turned his huge head, regarding Aryn with intelligent, and very bored, eyes. "He doesn't approve of this trip. Not a pack horse." She poked out her lip and affected a sulky tone, mimicking the elvish stallion's mental tones as he bemoaned his plight.

His eyes lingered, very briefly on her mouth before he smiled. "Bored, eh?" Aryn asked. Running an admiring eye over the lines of the steed, he agreed, "He's no pack horse. That's one of the finest animals I've ever seen."

Kilidare preened, tossing his head and lifting his feet high, prancing along the roadside as though it were a stadium.

"That'll keep him happy for a while," Tyriel said, laughing as Kilidare's neck arched. If he were a man, he'd be flexing his muscles about now, she mused.

"Tyriel."

She looked up, and nodded as Aryn gestured to the side with his head. Sometime later, they rode at the back of the train, far enough back that dust didn't disturb them, but close enough that they could be seen, if they were needed.

"I want to know more about…Irian," he finally said, scowling. Aryn had never been one for naming his sword, or anything other than his horse. And now, he was talking about the damn sword as if it were real.

"It is real. He is real."

Aryn's head flew up, eyes narrowed. "I don't care for anybody's hands inside my head," he said, coldly.

"Neither do I. And I wasn't in your head. I knew what you were thinking just from the look on your face." Cocking her head, she asked, "How old do you think I am?"

When he didn't answer, Tyriel sighed and turned her head away. She didn't care for the distrust she could see in his eyes. "I'm nearing my first century, Aryn. You don't spend that much time around humans without learning to read their expressions. I don't need to go poking into their minds; their thoughts are usually spread all over their faces.

"And for the record, I can't see into your head. I can pick up random emotions from time to time and I can speak with certain animals, and I do have some limited thought sensing. But it is very limited. I have to have some sort of bond with the person I am reading."

Now if you want to open your bed to me, we may be able to develop such a bond. Tyriel turned her own eyes away. She'd never been able to hide her expressions and feelings the way her elvin kin could.

A sigh drifted to her and she turned her head, meeting Aryn's eyes. "My apologies, Tyriel. I'm not thinking very clearly right now." Pressing one finger to his temple, he added, "Today has been rather disconcerting."

She nodded her understanding before saying, "I don't know much more than I've already told you. I didn't even know his name until I saw your sword earlier. It's my guess he either forced his soul into the blade, or it was trapped there. He may not even know the answer."

"How do you know it's old?"

"He, not it." Nodding her head to the forest to the east, she said, "I know he's old the same way you know those trees are old. Age leaves a mark, a feeling. And he is ancient. He's a predecessor of my gypsy kin, a race who called themselves Jiupsu—when he spoke to me, he recognized me, called me Jiupsu, the warriors that sing and dance."

"I don't want anything controlling me, ancient or otherwise."

With a smile, Tyriel lifted her face to the sky. "How did I know you were going to say that?" Her long braid trailed down her back and a tiny smile curved her lips. "How did I know?"

* * * * *

Aryn eyed the blade he held with acute dislike. He had a gut instinct that the feeling was mutual at this point. Heaven and hell, he'd gone crazy. He had acknowledged, if only to himself, that this hunk of metal had feelings.

Worse, it had a soul.

Aryn could sense that, just the way he could sense the being's displeasure at not being able to prod Aryn in going blindly in the direction he chose. Baring his teeth at the blade, he hoped the thing had finally gotten the point.

Aryn wasn't sure if he could take another morning like the past, should the blade not have gotten the point.

Around sunrise, for no reason, Aryn had decided he was fed up with the wagon train, fed up with Tyriel's instruction, bossy shrew that she was, and tired of sleeping on the ground.

He wanted a warm meal, a warm bed, and a warm woman next to him that night. He needed to fuck, he needed to drink, and he needed to not follow any person's orders but his own.

It wasn't until Tyriel appeared at his side while he packed up his supplies that he had questioned that nagging voice in his head.

"You signed a contract, swordsman. Doesn't that mean something to you?" she asked in a low voice.

He had started to snap at her, but then, her hand had landed on his arm and he had felt compelled to look her in the eye.

When he had done that, when he had looked into her oddly glowing amber eyes, the other compulsion shattered and fell apart. She had waited until the anger started to gather in his eyes before she had stepped back.

"He's done this to you before, I think," Tyriel had told him.

"You're his only link to the world now. He lives through you," she told him, holding the blade to keep him from hurling it off the cliff as they passed. "Throwing him off the cliff may work for a little while...but all it will do is have somebody picking him up long enough for the blade to drive that person insane while they deliver the blade to you. And you'll pay the price meanwhile. You're soul-bonded."

Through gritted teeth, he asked, "Is there a way to keep him from taking me over like that? *Those* weren't *my* thoughts, damn it. Yeah, a fuck would be nice, and so would a nice soft bed. But I've never neglected a contract and I'm not starting now!"

Her strong, deceptively slim shoulders raised in a shrug. "Only one way to find out." She returned the blade to him.

The moment she did, the urging was on him again. And when he resisted, it hurt. Like a fire was burning inside his head.

Irian wasn't happy at being refused.

His refusal, his thoughts were words, yet not like the compulsion he put into Aryn's mind, just urgings, feelings, anger. But they were real. The damn Soul in the sword was real.

Tyriel chuckled sometime later when Aryn nearly collapsed on the roadside. Taking pity on him, she had taken the sword, chiding the ancient being to be kinder to his wielder. The feelings she received in response had her blushing all the way to the roots of her hair.

If she ever had any doubt that he had once been mortal, all doubts died in that very moment. The force of his desire was enough to have Tyriel yearning for a cold bath.

The moment she laid her palm on the sword, touched her flesh to the metal that was oddly warm, pulsing as though it had a heartbeat, a wash of desire poured over her, a man's desire, and her mind was flooded with pictures. A man — the flickering image of that warrior, tall, rugged, with windblown black curls that tumbled down his back, and wicked black eyes—laying her down on a pile of furs and pillows, crushing her beneath him as he lifted her hips and buried his cock, thick and long, deep inside her body as she screamed and whimpered.

Oh, my.

She also knew that was the exact reason Aryn followed her into the woods later that night, why he had pinned her up against a tree trunk and kissed her the way she had been dreaming of since the moment she had first laid eyes on him. His wide-palmed, long-fingered hands buried themselves in her hair and held her still while he broke the seam of her lips with his tongue and feasted on her mouth like she was a fine, rare confection.

Aryn had tasted like the earth, the wind, the trees, and the sun...delicious, exotic, and like a man, something she had been craving for months. But *he* wasn't truly the one who was kissing her.

It was Irian who had followed her into the woods after she had risen sleepless from her bedroll, her head aching, her eyes heavy, and her mood edgy. Aryn, she would have sensed.

Irian...she never did.

Irian, in his rough, primal hungers, who had sensed her and hunted her down, a hungry, feral smile on his mouth as he slipped up behind her and slid his hands up her sides, whispering in her ear, "*Avet*, Tyriel, so sweet, so hot, I ache."

She knew that. It was why he was here.

It was why he had removed both their clothes in only seconds and went to his knees in front of her and lapped at her pussy until her cream flowed. Why he had taken her to the ground and thrust his heavy cock inside her body, why he had ridden her all night long.

Tyriel threw her head back and sobbed out Aryn's name, trying to call to *him* as Irian screwed two fingers in and out of her wet sheath before dragging her to the forest floor on the bed made of their clothes, shoving her thighs wide and burying his face between them again. *"My name…say my name,"* a deep, husky voice crooned inside her head. *"Scream it, wild little elf."*

The Soul in the sword…he had come out of his resting place with a fiery vengeance.

"Damn you, Irian," she seethed as she fisted her hands in Aryn's golden hair and rocked her hips up, cursing her own weakness.

"Damn me?" he purred against her, as he nuzzled her clit. Lifting up, he rested his chin on her pelvis, and Tyriel shuddered, staring into those black eyes, unable to focus on the face she knew she *should* see. Irian…it was Irian she was seeing. *"Avet,* sweet Tyriel, hot, tasty little elf…I am already damned." Lowering his face, he lifted her hips in his hands and plunged his tongue inside her wet folds, growling hungrily and lapping at her as though he were starved. "Damned t' only have a woman when he takes one, and so rarely do I have one like you…wet, wild, so full of magick ye make me heart ache as badly as m' cock." He shifted and drove two thick, long fingers inside her and she screamed, twisting up against him as she came.

A deep throbbing growl rose from his lips and he moved up her body, plunging his cock deep inside her. A wavy image shifted and formed in front of her eyes—a man, taller, broader, with long hair, black and wildly curly

as her own, black gypsy's eyes, a sensual mouth—
"Irian...my name is Irian and I am the man inside you, say my name," he insisted.

She shook her head, focused her eyes on the man's face above her, the sculpted lines of it, not the rougher hewn features of a long ago warrior, and wrapped her fingers in Aryn's hair, pulling his mouth down to her, praying in the morning she'd forgive herself.

She didn't particularly care if she forgave the enchanter trapped inside the blade or not.

His mouth possessed hers, and the taste of it was Aryn, like his scent, woodsy, male, and so addictive Tyriel was certain she'd die if this was the only time she would ever have a taste. The thick head of his cock stroked over the bundled bed of nerves buried by the mouth of her womb and she sobbed against his lips, feeling one big hand lift her up, holding her higher, harder against him as he shafted her, caressing her clit with each downward stroke.

She screamed against his mouth as her sheath tightened around him, going into spasms as she climaxed. His cock stiffened and jerked, pumping jets of hot seed deep inside her while she mewled and bucked underneath him, whimpering out Aryn's name.

While the angry man inside Aryn's body snarled, "Irian! Contrary little elf..."

She sighed, and then she laughed.

"You can take over his body from time to time. Even his mind for brief stretches. But not mine, Irian. Not mine."

Tyriel knew the need for physical release had been the only reason Aryn had so easily given into Irian's compulsion without even realizing he had done it. He was learning to recognize the Soul's touch, to question and block it.

He hadn't done any of it. Most likely because his own physical needs were so strong, part of him didn't *want* to question.

And if her own need hadn't been so overpowering, she could have easily brushed him aside, but it had been too long since she had felt a man's weight on her, too long since she had had a warm body beside hers in the night. And she had wanted him for what seemed like ages. If his own body hadn't hungered for a woman, any woman, maybe Irian wouldn't have been able to use that need against him.

The bloody bastard had used them, both of them.

And when morning came, the need had faded, and Aryn never had any memory of it.

She wasn't sure whether that was her doing, or Irian's. But within a matter of hours, she knew the night was lost to Aryn.

Watching him now, she waited patiently for the strain to enter his eyes, for the color to appear in his cheeks, the signs that Irian was once more testing his wielder.

It happened less often now.

Less often as in only five or six times a week, instead of five or six times a day.

When it did happen, the results could be anything from a headache, which had happened the first time — to a damn near collapse, which had happened just the previous night.

Something was calling to Irian, something on the other side of the chasm that lay just to the west as they left the woods of Morstia. Something more than the whim to live vicariously through Aryn.

But the blade had to learn a better way of communicating his needs and wants. And the enchanter was actually using words now instead of taking over Aryn—a first, she suspected.

And just now, whenever she made contact with him, Irian was unable to tell her why he wanted to go west. She had been unable to learn of anything through casting, and their contract would be fulfilled within two more weeks.

As she watched, the snarl faded from Aryn's face and he looked at her, that slight grin tugging at one side of his mouth. "He backed off. And what the bleeding hell do you know? The bastard can speak. He told me to go fuck myself, and a bloody arsed goat. They made them sick and twisted then, didn't they, elf?"

With an answering smile, she said, "Why doesn't it surprise me that you're just as stubborn as an ancient sword?"

They had to go, though. They fulfilled their contract easily enough, even finished within the week, with a bonus that they used to purchase new gear. Then Aryn mounted Bel and Tyriel mounted Kilidare and they rode like mad for Morstia. When they arrived, Aryn had a glittering look in his eyes, like a fever.

The small towne was almost picturesque in its perfection, with brightly colored cottages with thatched roofs on the outskirts, bricked buildings in the central section. Boys and girls were busily cleaning up the streets and guards were professionally friendly and courteous.

"And something is wrong here, ey?" Aryn drawled, kicking one long leg over Bel's back and sliding to the ground, his booted feet planted on the clean ground while he surveyed the neat little crowd of people surrounding him. "Wherever is the problem, you useless hunk of tin?"

Tyriel suppressed a smile and surveyed the streets. Oh, the towne was quite pleasant. And it wasn't a sham. She'd seen those kinds of townes before. This wasn't one. This was an out of the way little place, and likely they prided themselves on their cleanliness, their friendliness.

But...cocking her head, she scented the air, tasted it, felt it.

There was death here.

Not the normal death.

Bad death.

"The hunk of tin may have been right," she murmured, her eyes opening and scanning the crowd. They were drawn to a hand-lettered poster. In trader tongue, and in the language spoken in these parts, it read:

Missing

13 summers, female child

Elsabit Minsa

Last seen on Orsa Street near Sundown

On Midsummer Eve

REWARD

In the center of the poster was drawn a picture of a young girl, the bloom of innocence still on her face, caught by the artist's hand.

And beside it, the tattered remains of another poster.

And another.

Chapter Six

The constable studied the woman in front of him.

"Why should a gypsy and a swordsman care about our troubles?" he asked wearily, rubbing his grizzled face. *Oh, she was right. There were troubles, plenty of them. But what did outsiders know or care of them?*

Aryn opened his mouth, but Tyriel laid her hand on his arm and leaned forward, speaking in a low, soft voice. "I see the blood of the gypsy in you, Constable Chatre. You understand, don't you, when I speak of duty and right? You must, else you would not wear that symbol on your chest. I imagine, being of the gypsy folk, you know of the tales of a *geas*?

"We are under such thing," she said when he nodded slowly. "And we are honor bound by more than just that *geas*. What decent person would not wish to help? What decent person would not want to save innocent girls from whatever fate has befallen them?"

Chatre closed his eyes. "Honor bound? You speak of honor. So many have come and gone. Have none of them been decent folk?" He held up his hand when Tyriel would have spoken, shaking his head.

Long moments passed while he sat in silence, then a long, sad sigh filled the air.

"Four girls. Four in all, since last Midsummer's eve. And those are only the girls who are reported missing. We have very few homeless or beggar children, but they are here, like in any other towne. We know not how many of them have gone missing," the constable said slowly, sitting back in his chair and studying Tyriel with appraising eyes. "Gone without a trace, a scream, a sound. Nothing. Not a shred of clothing found, not a shoe, not a lock of hair. It's as though something swooped down out of the sky and made off with them."

They left after gathering what little information he could share, though he gladly shared what he could. Tyriel remembered it all without writing it down, nodding as she committed all to memory, what precious little he had to give.

"It's as though something swooped down out of the sky and made off with them," Chatre had said.

No. Someone in towne has them, she thought pacing up and down the streets, watching the people as they flowed around her and Aryn. And likely not dead at all. Dead bodies would be found.

And four or more dead bodies taken out of the city? No. Somebody would see them. Wagons taken out of the city tended to get inspected, even if just by dog. And a trained dog would set up a cry at the scent of a dead body. And you *could* take a body out through one of the smaller gates without a wagon, but still, likely somebody at sometime would have seen that.

"Tell me something," Aryn asked, sliding her a glance as they left the constable's office. "Why are you here? This has…nothing really to do with you. I can't shut out this voice in my head. But he doesn't hound you. He doesn't whisper to you of the voices he can hear crying for help."

Tyriel slowed her steps and cocked her head, a small smile playing at her lips. "I hear voices all on my own, Aryn. And I rather like you. I don't think I want to see you in too much hot water just because that sword won't leave you be." Lifting her eyes to the sky, the wind drifting through the air tickling her hair, she said quietly, "But I hear the voices as well. They call to me. And you and I can help them—I feel that in my gut."

They resumed walking, pausing here and there as Tyriel would stop to linger at a trinket booth, or to buy a sweet bun, smiling sweetly at a shopowner, her eyes twinkling brightly, her mind rapidly filing bits and pieces away as she asked nonsensical questions.

A young girl that used to sell pins. A minstrel...more missing girls.

"What are you thinking?" Aryn asked quietly as they paused in front of a particularly crowded inn.

She batted her lashes at him. Oozing female charm, she wrapped her hands around his biceps and pressed herself against his arm. "Perhaps the innkeeper would like to hire a swordsman with his lady mate. I'll serve the food. You can watch me while I do it," she cooed.

Aryn lifted a brow. "Any reason why he can't hire two? Or why we don't split up?" he drawled, keeping his voice low and backing her up against the wall, bending down as though to whisper intimately in her ear. The problem was, doing that brought her entirely too close. And she smelled rather unique. Far too good for his liking—far too female, far too sweet, and he had been so damn hungry for a taste. But they had been working together, still were. And Aryn didn't fuck swordmates. It never fared well.

Oh, but he wanted a taste of this sweet thing…

But why did she smell and feel so familiar? Something about the feel of her body against his seemed familiar, like he had lain against her before, smelled her before, tasted her before, fucked her, held her quivering body against his while she screamed against his mouth in climax.

"I'd rather nobody know too much about me just yet," she murmured, turning her head to whisper in his ear. The warm caress of her breath on his skin felt almost as intimate as if she had run her hands over his body and he gritted his teeth as his cock swelled in response.

"Excellent point," he agreed, straightening and trying to think in logistical terms instead of lustful ones. If they kept her gifts quiet, that meant a weapon none knew about. She had already wrapped and stowed her blade, and none could possibly imagine how many numerous weapons she had hidden on her person.

Aryn swore silently.

He imagined he could find them — piece by piece as he stripped her naked. The dusky gold of her skin gleamed richly and she winked at him as they crossed over the threshold.

"*Pretty thing, the Jiupsu women have always been lovely,*" Irian rumbled in the back of his mind. "*Take her upstairs…touch her, taste her.*"

"Shut up, you hunk of metal," Aryn warned. "Or I will wrap you in silk and stow you under the bloody bed."

Irian laughed. "*Willna do ye much good now. You've opened your mind to me. Close me out, you can, but removing me from your body does nothing,*" the ancient man said, his voice rich with amusement. Aryn could feel Irian watching Tyriel saunter through the tables, her hips swaying seductively as she tossed her hair and smiled flirtatiously at the innkeeper who was finishing up business with a vendor. *"Too long since we've had a woman, Aryn. And you've never known one like her, addictive as mead, rich as honey, spicy and hotter than fire…let's have her now."*

Aryn's blood pounded heavily in his cock, his head. He already ached, but Irian's seductive voice was making it worse, and Tyriel wasn't helping as she acted totally unlike herself, propping her tight little butt on a bench and leaning back on her hands, displaying her lithe, muscled form and firmly rounded breasts. The innkeeper smiled and nodded at them both and said, "Be with ya in a minute or so, folks. Have a seat, sirrah."

He continued to stand, but he moved closer to Tyriel, looming over her, drawing the scent of her skin into his nostrils, shuddering as it filled his head. *"She will taste so much better than she smells, brother of my soul,"* Irian promised. *"Come…"*

Tyriel went stiff, sitting up slowly, and turning her head, the playful twinkle dying from her eyes as she met Aryn's gaze. Irian's eyes. Her nostrils flared and Aryn could smell the scent of her arousal as she detected his. But she said slowly, her voice deeper and full of the power that filled her, "You are not yourself, Aryn."

"I am." Granted, his head did feel a bit…crowded, but he had wanted her for weeks, months…sometimes it seemed his entire life.

She blinked, once, slowly, then said softly, "Enchanter, you hold much sway over his mind right now. I feel it."

Aryn shook his head in confusion as she lapsed into a lyrical tongue—gypsy—but too archaic for him to follow. He felt Irian's rage, his refusal, his will trying to rise up. Pictures that didn't make sense filled his mind—Tyriel, lying on the forest floor while he spread her thighs, her woman's flesh, and ate from her sex as she screamed out his name, him moving to cover her, riding her hard, while the ghost of another man tried to come between them. Him—his body, Aryn of Olsted, touching her, tasting her, but he had never lain with her.

But why did it feel like memory and not fantasy?

Irian reared up, tried to force Aryn out, fighting him. He wanted to grab the half-elf, drag her upstairs—ah, hell—the fighting of the enchanter was not easy when the pictures he conjured were so close to what Aryn wanted right now as well. His cock still ached, but the vicious aching inside his head intensified as he battled Irian back and tried to retain control over his body and his mind.

"*Eyastian*, Irian. *Myiori, tymio efavo.*" Tyriel's voice came like a soft, cool breeze, full of comfort, full of power.

"*You would not dare,*" Irian growled, his rage thick, hot and coating everything Aryn stared at with a red film. "*You break our law by even speaking to me so, woman. I am Irian Escari, High Priest of the Jiupsu, Enchanter, Swordsman. You would not dare—*"

"I would. Times have changed since you walked the world, enchanter. I am not of your clan. The Jiupsu are now the gypsy and they do not follow the laws of the dominant. I owe you no fealty. And even if I did...I am only half-gypsy. The other half is elvish Princess. A Princess of the kin would be your equal, High Priest, not your submissive." A brow lifted and she smiled coolly. "And can you truly see me submitting to any man? An elf? Even back in your time, I imagine the kin followed their own rules," she whispered as she rose and stood staring Aryn in the eyes. But it was not Aryn she was facing.

It was Irian, who was trying once more to throw Aryn to the sidelines and take over his body. He saw the swordsman as weaker, as the submissive and felt Aryn's body should rightfully belong to him. After all, Aryn had no true magick to call his own. He was mortal, and therefore, in the eyes of so many of the earlier races, weaker than the magicked people.

"If that were truly the case, don't you think that by now you would have destroyed Aryn completely?" she asked. "But it is still his body."

"*A good lad. No reason he can't be around. Sometimes,*" Irian sneered.

"His body. You try to steal it. The gypsies are an honest people. I would have thought the Jiupsu were as well," Tyriel said thoughtfully, cocking her head. "But I meant what I said. *Myiori, tymio efavo.* Do you wish to see if we can?"

And just like that, the enchanter withdrew his presence, and Aryn was alone in his body once more.

"I can fight my own battles," Aryn growled, his cheeks flushing red.

She cocked a brow. "I'm well aware. But I was merely informing him that I would offer you a weapon to rid yourself of him if he persisted in trying to own you," she said simply, sitting back down, as if unaware of the tense state of his body.

Aryn wished he wasn't aware.

He could still smell her, damn it, still taste the scent of her arousal lingering on the air, and he wondered if maybe he shouldn't have just given into the bastard, at least a little.

"What weapon?" he asked cautiously as he moved around the table and settled into the seat, staring into her face.

For mere moments, her eyes seemed to glow again, like they had in the inn that day they had first met. And she softly whispered, "Myself."

Tyriel was relieved when Aryn left the room to her just a little later. She hated using any kind of persuasion, so she hadn't. But something told her Irian had. They had gotten just the job they had needed a touch too easily, and a room, a private one to boot. Granted, the tiny little enclave under the stairs wasn't much, but it had a door, a bed, and it was clean, quiet, and private.

She suspected the private was something Irian wanted a great deal.

Keep dreaming, you enchanted hunk of metal, she taunted as she lowered herself onto the narrow bed. It was just large enough for two. If you liked your bedmate. Reaching up, she stroked the amber moonstone at her neck with a sigh. *Oh, Da...I've really gotten myself into a mess this time.*

Daughter mine, that is what you have always done best, Josah, High Prince of the Elvin Realm of Eivisa whispered to her lovingly. And the moonstone glowed warm under her hand.

She smiled and lay back, closing her eyes.

And then she reached out.

Blackness.

Such blackness.

She had never encountered such evil. In all her years, she had met many people, and many of them had been twisted, wretched souls without a drop of goodness in them. The evil swarmed up and tried to seek her out, claim her. It touched her and she shrieked, drawing back from it. Her breath caught in her chest and in desperation, she wrapped one hand around the chains at her neck, seeking out not the moonstone, but the crucifix, whispering softly, and jerking herself out of the mire of evil magick as she flung herself from the bed, landing painfully hard on her ass.

Cleansing, purifying gypsy magick rushed through her and the touch of the pendant at her neck grounded her. Faith, that was all it took. Just the reminder of faith, she told herself.

But the slimy feel that clung to her, suffocated her was unlike anything she had ever encountered. Tyriel opened her eyes and lay staring at the ceiling, panting and gasping for breath. Whoever he was, he had shielded himself but it would not matter to her.

A sorcerer, perhaps, or another blood mage. He hadn't acted recently, and that was all that had kept her from finding him. The kind of blood magick he practiced was not the kind that could hide from an elemental mage such as herself. The blood would sink into the earth, stain it, mark it and it would call to her.

It had been some time, so it would not be long before he struck again.

* * * * *

Aryn settled into a corner, looking foreboding and somber, his pale hair pulled back in a queue, Irian strapped at his back, a sleeveless leather jerkin revealing the long, powerful muscles in his arms, veeing halfway down his chest. From time to time, he would glance at Tyriel and smile, or glare at the men who slid her long, lingering glances, but for the most part, he remained silent. Looking grim, possessive, and serious was his role.

Being flirtatious and empty-headed was hers.

Both were doing a very good job.

The elf was gathering...feelings. She had sensed something the past night, Aryn knew. She wouldn't tell him what. And he didn't feel right in pushing. She was here helping him—she didn't have to be here.

He, on the other hand, did. Irian no longer compelled him. There was a gnawing in his gut, some dark evil that lingered at the edges of this small, perfect little towne that was trying to destroy it.

"Stop it, lad," Irian said with a sigh. He had the disturbing image of another man, a bit taller, broader, thick, wildly curling hair, black gypsy's eyes—the man seemed to be standing beside him, watching Tyriel as

intently as Aryn did. *"She does have t' be here. She feels the same gnawin' in her gut tha' ye are feelin' right now. Her heart compels her t' be here the same as does yours."*

Aryn shifted against the wall and muttered, "I liked it better when you were just a sword."

Irian laughed. *"Never was I just a sword, Aryn. And well ye know it. Part of ye has always known."* The ghost-like image of Irian that lingered in Aryn's mind seemed to shift and he propped one fur-lined boot against the wall, watching as a man lifted his mug of ale to his lips and drank while watching Tyriel with hot hungry eyes. *"He is wondering if she's for hire. Not from here. Gettin' ready t' toss some coin her way for a quick fuck."*

Aryn quirked an eyebrow at that. "Is he now?" he murmured. "Apparently my possessive act needs a bit of work."

Irian glanced over at him. *"Lad, if ye only knew...he's a bloody fool. Everybody else knows t' whom she belongs."* The ghostly image slid him a narrow look. *"Well, almost. But he's daft and stupid. And Tyriel is a lovely, hot young thing, he thinks, and good for no' much more than a hard fucking. And he's monied. He thinks that's all tha' matters."*

Aryn watched through slitted eyes as Tyriel returned with a fresh mug of ale and a bowl of stew for the man in question. He slid a hand up the outside curve of her hip with one hand, brandished a palmful of silvers with the other, nodding toward the stairs.

Tyriel smiled and shook her head.

As she started to turn away, he closed his hand more tightly around her hip, dropped the silvers, and reached for her, jerking her onto his lap. "*Stupid,*" Irian repeated as Aryn shoved away from the wall. "*Verra, verra stupid.*"

"That's my lady you're handling there, man," Aryn said in a low growl, clamping his hand down on the back of the trader's neck and squeezing hard in warning. "Unless you want to leave this towne with bloody stumps at the end of your wrists, and a bloody hole where your cock once hung, then I suggest you let her go."

Tyriel was fighting not to laugh as she moved smoothly off the man's lap. Aryn was aware how easily she could have gotten away, but not many of those ways would have let her keep her helpless guise up.

"Now," Aryn purred silkily, jerking the man up off the bench and turning, whirling on his heels and slamming the stuttering trader into the wall. "Perhaps we should establish rules of etiquette."

"*He speaks so pretty for a swordsman,*" Irian said laughingly.

Tyriel had to turn, and Aryn suspected the shuddering of her shoulders was suppressed laughter, but it looked from the corner of his eye like she was crying. "Oh, now I'm truly pissed—my lady is distraught." Aryn jerked the man forward and slammed him back again so that his head rapped the wall.

"I didna know she had a man!" the trader bellowed. He started to shove Aryn away, but Aryn drew the long, wicked blade at his side and pressed it to the trader's throat. "Bloody hell, she sashays around here, twitching her ass, bending over and letting men see her damn tits. What else are we to think?"

"That she is a friendly maid servant trying to do her job well and earn good tips?" he answered. "No other dared to touch her. If your cock needs a pussy, then go find the Whore's Guild. You entered through the Towne Gates the same as we. You should have read the posting. No whoring in the taverns. No whoring in the inns. Period. It would have been bad enough if you had touched *any* of the barmaids in here, but you touched mine."

Aryn wondered fleetingly if he was getting too much into his act here. But then he sheathed his knife and plowed his fist into the trader's belly, before delivering an elbow to his jaw and sending him crashing to the floor. After deciding he was well and out, he carried him out into the street and threw him down into the dirt.

"Hope a bloody pickpocket makes off with your wealth," he said as he strode back into the inn and made his way to his 'lady'. She was still 'crying' and distraught and none of the other barmaids could get her to look up or calm down.

Aryn wrapped his arms around her, lowering his head before he rolled his eyes and murmured into her mass of curls, "Don't you think you're carrying on a bit much?"

She snickered, forcing it into a fake sob as she wrapped her arms around him. "My lady? You touched my lady..." she whispered, snickering against his chest as he stroked one hand soothingly down her back and wished she would control her giggles before he lost his control and kissed her right there.

Adorable, sweet, sexy as all get out—damn it—he wanted to eat her up in one greedy bite. And Tyriel was giggling her cute little ass off.

Aryn had the disturbing image of Irian watching them. This time, with something that looked like envy in his black eyes.

Aryn lay on his belly on the bed late that night, with Tyriel on her side, spooned up against him. She slept silently, occasionally sighing or humming softly in her sleep as she dreamed whatever a magickal thing such as she dreamed.

Her scent filled his head and the feel of her skin seemed forever embedded on his hand—and his cock ached. How in the hell was he supposed to do this—sleep in a bed with a beautiful woman, and not touch her?

But a wild half-gypsy, half-elf seemed untouchable, so out of reach. She would live centuries—was already nearing her first. She had the power of divine beings running through her, and she called the two most mystical, most feared races in all of Ithyrian her blood kin. The elves and the gypsies.

And Aryn of Olsted was not going to insult her by asking if he could sate his hunger for a woman by fucking her.

"It is not just a hunger for any woman, ye daft fool. Ye ache and hunger for her."

Aryn tried to ignore the whisper in his mind, but it was like ignoring the pressure in his loins, or the feel of her against him, near impossible.

No matter how much he may wish to at the moment.

"It is no insult if she wants it," Irian groused.

"Go to sleep."

"I'm dead, remember? Little good sleep does me. I'll rest when you do, lad. And a good fuck would help us both," he suggested slyly. As Aryn stared at the wall, Irian started to flicker into view, a little more in focus this time than he had been earlier. Aryn closed his eyes, but a sharp afterimage remained.

"Why in the name of the Holy Fire am I seeing you now?" he demanded irritably.

Irian tossed him a wolfish grin that seemed to glow in the dim room. *"Wouldna ye like t' know?"* he taunted.

"If I didn't want to know, I wouldn't have asked," Aryn muttered irritably.

"Would you two be quiet and let me sleep?" Tyriel said into the silence. "I do not know what you two are carrying on about but I hear your voices in the back of my head and it's quite bothersome."

Aryn thanked the Sacrificed God she hadn't been able to pick out the words of the conversation.

And Irian chuckled before fading into silence.

Aryn developed a reputation for being a very possessive husband, but one who strayed. Tyriel was thankful there was no true bond between them because as the days turned into weeks, he developed a habit of leaving their room at night, and in such a small inn, his comings and goings could not go unnoticed.

And since his first visit was with the sister of one of the barmaids, Tyriel had the pleasure of learning about it. Not directly...the people in this inn were actually very kind. But with her kind's sharp hearing, she heard it well enough as she passed down the hall.

Tyriel had already known there had been women — hearing names only added salt to the wound. She had smelled the woman and the sex on his skin as he came into the room, though he had bathed well. And if she wasn't mistaken, she had heard a disgruntled sigh slither through the air. Irian wasn't pleased with his wielder.

Tyriel was a bit displeased herself. And a bit hurt. After more than a month of the same treatment, it was only getting more painful. She was fighting an attraction to the sexy swordsman that just would not fade away and if he would just turn his midnight eyes her way —

"Bloody hell," she hissed. In a fit of rage, she spun a dancing ball of fire in her hands, a harmless illusion, and then she lobbed it at the wall, watching it break and shatter into nothingness. "Bloody hell."

Blood.

Hell.

Blood magick.

Painful slow death and sacrifice to the darkness below.

Burning, strong bonds came lashing out to bind her. Tyriel struck out, flinching as more magick swelled up out of the darkness.

She felt something reach out and grab her and she struck out, shielding automatically, flinging true fire at her assailant and feeling him flinch and bellow out in pain. She launched herself at him instinctively and searched…for just an instant…

Chapter Seven

Tyriel was polishing Irian when Aryn came through the door in the early morning on their day off. He spotted her and frowned. "That isn't necessary," he said.

Sliding him a neutral glance, she responded, "It is if I want to speak with the enchanter and you aren't available. How are the houses in the Whore's Guild? Finding them to your liking?"

He cocked a brow at her. "There's a variety to choose from. Hard not to find one to my liking. They've men as well, if you've a need."

She smiled a slow cat's smile and said coolly, "I do not pay for sex, swordsman. If I have a need, I would handle it myself. Or find my own partner. But that is not why I ask."

She watched as Irian flicked into view now that his bearer was there. She stood staring at the man who had used Aryn's body to take her and felt the sadness nearly overwhelm her. He wanted her. This man who was long dead. Aryn so clearly did not. "The enchanter and I have been...discussing the situation. I had a problem of sorts when I did a bit of magick. Small, very small, but something seemed to have been waiting for it and tried to grab me. He failed, miserably, and I got an idea of what and where he was."

"And what, pray tell, does the Whore's Guild have to do with this?" Aryn asked, confused, looking from Tyriel to Irian.

"How do you feel about bloodsport in your sex, brother?" And the enchanter proceeded to fill Aryn in on what Tyriel had learned.

* * * * *

Aryn's stomach was roiling.

His entire body shook with rage, yet he felt slightly ill.

Staring at Tyriel's face, Aryn thanked the Holy Fire Irian had finally gone silent.

After what Irian had relayed, he wanted little more than to race down the streets and find the house she spoke of. And kill. Murder. Maim. Mutilate.

"Aye, and slowly," Irian purred as he paced the room. *"But it isna time."*

"At moon dark, Aryn. Only at moon dark," Tyriel said quietly. "The mage was looking for a new offering. He has been looking ever since the past new moon last week. That one was a slave child one of his followers brought from outland. He feels safe in taking another from the streets here again."

"And he was thinking on taking you," Aryn guessed.

She laughed without humor, her amber eyes cold and wintry. "A bad thought, that. I imagine he is still regretting it." Her head cocked and she closed her eyes. A smile, one almost sexual in its nature crossed her face as a small shiver raced through her body. "I can still taste his pain. Rarely does such a thing bring me pleasure."

"But this did."

"Like fine wine," she said, raising her lids slowly and meeting Aryn's gaze levelly, her mouth curving into a small, sated smile that had his blood heating. "I know his scent now, his blood, his feel. He cannot hide from me."

"But he will know you as well."

"No. He was too busy seeing me as prey to realize I was the hunter. He knows nothing about me, save that I have a magick that he wants badly. He felt magick and struck, thinking that I was weak and helpless. To him, all others are weak and helpless. He felt power, saw power, wanted power. So he tried to take it." For a brief moment, she had wanted to run, to flee this nasty insidious evil that had tried to creep inside her—she longed for the woods, the plains, the mountains, for their purity and splendor.

For home.

Eivisa.

But first—there was a battle to win, an enemy to fight. A warrior in her heart, she had to answer the call she heard inside and find and destroy this evil. It felt like it had crawled underneath her skin and dug in, planted itself there, filthy, malignant, and growing. "He will come looking for me. I could let him find me—I suspect I can handle him." A feral gleam lit her eyes and had Aryn wondering exactly what skills she had that she didn't reveal. "Or I could continue to hide and if he doesn't find me, he will look for another offering."

"An offering to what?" Aryn asked softly.

"The Darkness Below," she whispered. "He gathers power, harvests it from the young ones he kills. He takes the ones who have some sort of gift, be it healing or enchantment or even a touch of herb witchery. Any sort of magick will suit his purpose."

"And there is also the brothel he runs — the ones he doesna kill, he breaks and they serve there it would seem," Irian added softly, his voice gruff with sympathy for the girls.

"So why are we standing here talking about it instead of killing him?" Aryn asked, his voice rough and deep with rage. He held out his hand for his blade and Tyriel offered it with a lifted brow and a bow of her head. He closed his hand around the pommel, feeling his fingers settle familiarly around the curves and grooves, like an extension of himself. As he touched the blade, he felt Irian's own rage. It felt like coming home, oddly, or like the other half of his own soul as he donned the sheath and settled the blade in position down his back.

Tyriel continued to sit on the bed with her legs folded, her long narrow feet bare, a slim gold ring around her second toe winking at him in the dim light as she studied him with calm, appraising eyes.

"Aryn, if we go in there and kill him, be it with steel or with magery, you and I will be risking our necks. Now, it may just be, literally, a pain in the neck for me. But it would good and well kill you. And if my Da hears of a bunch of mortals laying hands on me for trying to help them, tsk, tsk, tsk, do we really need the army of the elvin kingdoms raining down on the mortals?" she asked, unfolding her legs and shifting to lie on her side, stretching her long legs out and crossing them at the ankle. "Da would be well and truly pissed, and I wouldn't be very happy myself. And the gypsies would go quite insane once they heard of it. It would be mayhem."

"Oh, then we ignore it?" he asked sarcastically.

"No," she drawled, lifting her gaze skyward as if praying for patience. She took a deep breath that strained the laces of her chemise and Aryn wished she had bothered to don a little more than that and her breeches as her nipples pressed against the cloth, the peaks taunting him to madness. "We gather proof. And we let...reinforcements arrive. He is not alone. He has at least two other mages. I am good, quite good. But I am not stupid. And Irian, beg your pardon, there is only so much you can do without a body to call your own."

"If the stubborn swordsman would let me use his — "

"It's the stubborn swordsman's body," Aryn said stubbornly.

"And he has a right to it," Tyriel agreed. "And I think we should establish that now. Can you offer your bond to no longer try to take over his body simply at your own behest?"

"I took a vow at my death, lady of the Jiupsu. Do you no longer honor vows?" Irian growled.

"We honor them. But you do not honor your wielder when you force your will on him," she said coolly. "I understand your vow, better than you would think. It was a noble thing you did, I believe. But trying to force a man out of his body is not an act of honor."

Irian was silent. And then grudgingly, *"No more forcing my will at my own...behest,"* he grunted. *"But when the need arises..."*

"Your version of need had better have been revised very recently," Tyriel said softly, an edge to her voice.

Aryn stared at her, hard. And then he turned his head, searching for the flickering form of Irian, but the man had not reformed again. In the back of his mind, he heard Irian's voice, but not his words, and watched as Tyriel lowered her lashes in acknowledgment, but no words were spoken out loud. *"I think there's something going on that I need to know about,"* he said to Irian.

"Nay. Ye need not know," Irian said. *"My bond has been given. I'll not be forcin' my will on ye. But ye must be understandin'. My vow, I canna break, not now, not until I am no more."*

"Bloody hell, you stupid piece of tin, I'm here, aren't I?" Aryn snapped, resisting the urge to take the blade off and fling it against the wall. It wouldn't hurt the enchanter any and worse, he knew better than to treat a weapon like that.

"Exactly what sort of proof do we need?" he asked slowly, lowering himself to the floor, shifting Irian to an angle and staring at Tyriel with hard eyes. "And why do I get the feeling you're going to send me to this house?"

She smiled nastily. "Have you any idea how many times I've heard 'poor Tyriel', or worse—'she must not be very good in bed if he has to wander so much'. Look at it this way, darling. You owe me," she purred, batting her lashes at him. "Otherwise we could have waited until Jaren arrived."

"Jaren?"

"Backup," she answered. Her amber eyes gleamed. "One of my father's men. An elvish...you would probably call him an assassin. He was one of my teachers. He will be here come morning. But you will sort of wander into the house tonight, have a drink, look slightly interested but embarrassed and then wander out."

* * * * *

Aryn stood at the bar, unimaginatively painted black, and drank his ale. A slim little whore who looked to be all of eighteen, stood at his elbow, trying to coax him upstairs, offering to let him 'discipline' her in any fashion he chose. She wore nothing but heavy gold rings pierced through her nipples.

And her eyes were frightened.

Frightened. Almost all of the girls here were frightened, frightened and broken. Aryn was all but sick with it. This poor girl, he wanted to take her away and find her a safe place, some clothes to wrap around her slender body, wash away the paint they had applied to her face.

She didn't want to be here.

So far, he hadn't seen a single woman who actually looked pleased about where she was.

And the men looked all too pleased to have a woman under their hands to break, a woman they could make submit and yield and humiliate.

He wanted badly to take her out of there, but Tyriel's words lingered.

And something eating in his gut stopped him as well.

There was something else going on here besides a whorehouse.

Something dark and evil that left a bad taste in his mouth and a sick feeling in his gut. And if he took this sad little waif out of here, it would destroy his chance of helping to figure out what. So he told her no, trying to act as though he was just checking it out and offered her a flirtatious smile and said, "Maybe next time...?"

"Eira," she said with a sad smile before she left to go find somebody else. Only problem was, he had been the only one who didn't look at her like he'd enjoy hurting her.

Aryn blanked his face as he watched one of the patrons bend his whore over his lap and administer a spanking. He didn't exactly have a problem with spankings—but then the man stood and had her unfasten his breeches right there.

Now that, he had a problem with.

Especially when the young woman's face flamed with embarrassment and she started to shake and fumble as she realized how many people were watching her.

"Bloody hell," he muttered.

It only got worse when another man moved behind her and started to spank her as she started to suckle and lick on the man's cock, her cheeks hot with embarrassment.

"Anybody can cut in," a silken voice offered. "And if you pay...oh, twenty-five silvers, she's all yours. Of course, Eira would be disciplined since she offered for you first."

Aryn turned his head and met a pair of boldly painted blue eyes and a slicked red mouth. The woman staring at him had to be none other than the madam and she was dressed in a rather elegant evening gown. She dressed in rich clothing while her whores wore nothing.

Aryn set his ale down and started to decline, but then he saw the whip that was being pulled out. And he reached for his money belt instead. "How much for both?" he asked, sending the madam a smile.

He watched her eyes settle on his mouth and she hummed slightly. "I think I'd rather have you for myself," she purred. "Too bad I have a policy of never taking a customer to bed."

And so for the price of forty silvers, he had both lovely young women all to himself.

Aryn found himself staring into the eyes of two women who had more familiarity with rough usage than gentle, and he didn't know what the fuck he was supposed to do.

But he sure as hell couldn't touch them with the smell and sweat of other men all over them.

So he was shown to a rather opulent room and fed while the ladies were taken to bathe. One of the women moved to shove Eira and Aryn rolled out of his chair and caught her hand, smiling silkily. "I realize this is a house of pain and pleasure, but I've paid well for these ladies.

Any marks on them tonight will come from me, and only me. Otherwise, I mark you," he warned.

By the time they returned, he had decided to just leave. Slip them what little money he had left, and leave.

Eira took one look at his face and knew.

So did the other. Her name was Keely and she was a bit bolder than Eira. She moved like a spring storm, fast and light, sliding her arms around his neck and plastering herself to his front, cuddling her curvy little body against him and rocking. Then whispering, "They watch us, if you leave they'll know...they'll punish us."

Aryn froze. He lowered his head and caught her face as if to kiss her, nuzzling his way around and down to her ear where he asked, "What?"

She giggled flirtatiously, ran her hands over his shoulders, and said, "You don't belong in here. We both know that. But if you leave without fucking us, we get punished. We're being watched. It's one of the house entertainments."

Well, hell.

Threading his fingers through her hair, he licked and nuzzled his way down her torso to take one of her pierced nipples in his mouth, tugging delicately on the golden loop as Eira moved behind him and started tugging at his clothes. He ushered them to bed and thought fleetingly, *I know this isn't what Tyriel had in mind...*

And then he plunged his fingers into Keely's tight, narrow passage and listened to her squeal in startled delight and decided he'd been right. None of the patrons had ever given a damn about their pleasure.

So he worked his way down her body, spread her thighs and opened her, studying the smooth waxed flesh of her mound before lowering his face to her flesh and breathing in her scent—sweet and young, even if these bastards had broken her. She jumped when he opened her pussy and licked her, startled, she sobbed when he caught her clit in his mouth and worked it gently as he again slid two fingers inside her slippery sheath.

He felt her hands fist in his hair, heard her broken panting sighs as she lifted her hips eagerly against his mouth as he quickly brought her to orgasm before he pushed up and turned his eyes to Eira.

Her soft hazel eyes were glassy with surprised delight, and as he tumbled her into his lap, she gasped and threw her arms around his neck, arrowing in on his mouth and kissing him hungrily, mindlessly. Keely was soon at his back, sliding her hands between them, whimpering feverishly and jerking at the laces of his jerkin as he kissed Eira and slid his hand between her thighs to pet her naked mound.

She had been pierced through her clitoris. When her head lowered in shame, he knew it wasn't of her own choosing. If it had been, Aryn would have no problem with it, but having something so personal forced on a woman, and in such a tender spot… "Ah, you poor thing," he murmured, keeping his voice low. "I'll kiss it and make it better."

Aryn slid his tongue gently around the golden ring that ran through her clit and nuzzled her, taking the engorged flesh in his mouth in a gentle, suckling kiss that had the woman arching up off the bed against his mouth with a scream that echoed off the walls. Pumping his fingers in and out of her pussy, he waited until she was coming before he moved up her body and rose to his knees. Freeing his cock from his breeches, he came down on top of her, pushing inside her with one slow, deep thrust that had her lashes fluttering and a soft, low purr falling from her lips.

Falling into a slow, steady rhythm, he waited until she had climaxed before he moved away and reached for Keely, guiding her onto her hands and knees and driving deep inside her as Eira lay gasping for breath and smiling in blissful pleasure.

Tyriel waited until nearly midnight.

He hadn't yet returned from the house.

Clenching her jaw, she slid into bed.

"If ye would just na' be so stubborn, little elf, I could help —"

"I'm not touching you. There is no reason that you should be able to speak to me," she said coolly.

"I can speak t' ye at any time I choose, so long as ye are near," Irian murmured huskily as his body shimmered into view. He moved to lie beside her, studying her with dark, fathomless eyes. *"I can bring him t' ye, whenever ye want him."*

"Hardly. Because I only want him if he wants me in return," she said. "Leave me be." Then she rolled onto her side and wondered if maybe she shouldn't just pack up and head back to the Kingdoms with Jaren when he arrived.

"If you don't, at least once, they will wonder why you came at all," Eira whispered as she plastered herself against Aryn under the guise of kissing his neck.

Aryn's jaw was rigid, as it had been for the past half an hour. They had told him, repeatedly. It was expected that he tie up at least one of them, and spank them, or force one of them into submitting, or let the other woman spank or whip…something…to give credence to why he was interested in a house of painful pleasures.

If it wasn't for the fear in Eira's eyes, or the resignation in Keely's…aw, damn it all to hell. He tumbled Eira off his lap, and reached for Keely, shoving her to her knees in front of him and urging her mouth to his cock. She opened eagerly, her wide eyes locked on his face as he threaded his fingers through her hair and pushed his cock a little deeper.

"Eira, get the wrist bindings for your friend," he said gruffly, before he lost his nerve for this game.

'Twas a dangerous game they played. If he wasn't convincing, these two young women were likely to be beaten when he left. "Tie her wrists behind her back, then get the toy from the wardrobe, the glass one," he ordered, trying not to think about the eyes he knew were watching. He had spotted the spy holes. And his gut told him the mirrors over the bed weren't truly mirrors…not just mirrors anyway.

As Eira approached, her eyes nervous and hesitant on his face, he pushed her gently to her knees and said, "Fuck her with it."

Aryn watched, his heart stuttering in his chest despite himself as the mirrors afforded him a wonderful view of the thick golden glass dildo being slowly pushed inside Keely's tight's pussy. "More than that, Eira. Harder, make her moan," he ordered.

Glancing at Keely, he said, "You like that?"

Her eyes fluttered open and she nodded awkwardly as she slid her head up and down and swirled her tongue around the head of his cock. He pushed inside her mouth, grasping her hair and wrapping it around his fist, pushing deeper. "Suck on me, sweet, I like the way that mouth feels."

Keely gasped around his cock as the cool dildo pushed inside her swollen sex. She whimpered as Aryn pushed his cock deeper, nearing her limits, bruising her lips, her throat as he started to pump his hips, moving roughly back and forth inside the wet embrace of her mouth.

Eira plunged the glass dildo deep and high, staring wide-eyed as Keely deep-throated Aryn's cock and started to shudder. "Play with yourself, Eira. No need for you to get left out," Aryn teased, before looking back down and watching as his cock, red and wet slid back out of Keely's swollen mouth.

Her body was starting to shudder and her nipples were getting tighter, harder as her breathing picked up. "You want to come, don't you? No, love," he purred. "Can't have that. Not yet." Then he pulled away and bent Keely forward, gripping her hips in his big hands and driving deep inside her bound body, lifting one hand and smacking her ass sharply.

And through the mirror, those watching sighed, some in satisfaction, some in pleasure.

One with a bit of disappointment. The madam had been looking forward to punishing those girls.

* * * * *

She smelled it on him as he walked in, very early the next morning. Sex and sweat, rich, pungent. But something was different.

She smelled two different women.

With a snarl, she threw her legs over the side of the bed and stood, gathering her clothes and striding out of the room wearing nothing more than her hair and a sullen sulk while Aryn stood staring at her naked ass with bemused eyes, and wondered why the half-elf had been sleeping naked.

Jaren arrived later that morning.

Tyriel was wiping down a table when she felt his presence. And his anger. "Elvish Princesses do not act the menial," he hissed, standing rigid in the doorway.

If he hadn't had years and years of deference to her father bred into him, he probably would have crossed the space between them, jerked the cleaning rag from her and paddled her ass. Not that the last idea didn't hold a little bit of appeal. She turned her head slowly and winked at him.

Jaren Everess, Lord of Remme, one of the legendary De Asir, vengeance killers, narrowed his dark, glittering green eyes at her audacity. His skin was pale, almost translucent ivory that glowed against the emerald of his eyes. His high, arched brows, his carved cheekbones and pointed chin, all were the defining features of the beautiful elvish race.

But Jaren was...more.

Long and sleek muscled with thick wrists, broad shoulders and a chest that tapered down to an impossibly narrow waist and a tight ass that Tyriel had studied a number of times before. She had sighed quite dreamily over him a time or two in her youth, and while he had trained her in the halls of De Asir. Strong powerful thighs, muscled legs...hmmm, her mouth was watering. Up until she had met Aryn she had always thought Jaren was the most sensual, desirable man-creature she had ever met in her life.

He was certainly the most arrogant.

A muscle in his jaw ticked as he continued to stare at her, enraged that a Royal dared to clean a table.

And for mortals.

"Jaren don't be such an arrogant bore. I'm not doing anything that bothers me. Do not let it bother you," she said softly. "And stop acting so dangerous. You aren't supposed to attract too much attention."

The rigidity slowly left his shoulders and he forced the anger in his eyes to bank, but she could still feel the rage pumping off of him in waves. And something she had not felt in far longer than she cared to think about…desire. For her.

With a slow, pleased smile, she turned back to the task at hand as Jaren moved into the tavern and made his way to her table, shoving back his hood. He would act as though he were an old counterpart of Aryn's, and she would act surprised to see him.

And later…maybe she would do something about this aching in her loins. She allowed a slow, heated smile to curve her lips, and some of the heat to reflect in her eyes as he moved toward her.

His response sent a thrill of excitement racing through her, and need tightened in her belly, her cleft going hot and wet.

Jaren's lids lowered as he scented her, a slow, careful breath leaving him.

"What a very…pleasant surprise to see you," she said.

He took her hand, lifted it to his lips and kissed it. "The pleasure is all mine." His tongue slid out, caressing her hand before he released it.

Aryn was half asleep when Tyriel left the bed. She wore a white shift that ended just at her thighs and she smoothed it down, smiling a cat's smile as she slid her hands through her hair.

When she left the room in silence, he knew exactly where she was going. He saw the smile curving her lips and wanted to grab her, pin her against the wall and drive his cock inside her until she screamed out his name.

Until she forgot where she was going.

The elf's room.

The door closed behind her, leaving him with the image of her rounded, tight little ass and he groaned.

Jaren was a long, impossibly slim elf with straight, raven-wing hair that fell to his waist and eyes that glowed greener than a cat's. And like every other bloody elf Aryn had ever met in his life, he was as beautiful and sexual a creature as anything the Sacrificed God had ever created. His shoulders were wide and strong, arrogantly proud, tapering down to a narrow waist and long legs. His pointed ears he kept hidden by keeping his hood up. His skin was pale—pale as snow it seemed. He oozed danger and menace, unless he was looking at Tyriel and then he oozed loyalty and a fierce possessiveness that had Aryn wondering. And just the slightest bit jealous—which made no sense at all.

And he watched Tyriel with a hunger that seemed to match Aryn's. But Jaren would get to sate his appetite.

He closed his eyes and sighed grimly.

"Life sure as hell got complicated all of a sudden," he muttered.

"Life has always been complicated," Irian said with a sleepy chuckle as he roused long enough to puzzle out what had Aryn disgruntled. *"You've just now started t' live, thas' all."*

* * * * *

"Too long," he purred against her neck as he caught her hair in his hand and wound it around his fist. "Too long since I have touched you, held you, felt your sweet body against me."

Tyriel shuddered as his hands moved up from her waist, cupping her breasts, plumping them together, plucking the nipples, milking them, as he lowered his mouth to her neck and raked it with his teeth.

"I've been aching for the sight of you, the taste of you again, milady," he rasped, moving one hand down to her belly and pressing her back against him, cuddling his cock against her ass. "Dying inside from it."

She shuddered as he reached down and plunged two fingers inside her pussy, her knees nearly giving out beneath her. "Jaren—"

He laughed softly. "So you do remember my name," he teased. "I thought perhaps in your obsession with a mortal you had forgotten me."

"Jaren," she teased, wiggling her butt, leaning her head back against one broad, strong shoulder. Here, this was the one place, in all her years that she had always felt truly safe, truly desired, truly wanted. "Never forgotten. Hmmm, oh!" He flicked her clit with his thumb as he breathed a breath of magick down her body, sending hot little licks of illusory fire over her skin, playing with her nipples, teasing her.

"So you say now," he whispered somberly as he urged her to the bed, reaching for the back of her chemise.

It fell from her in shreds as he tore it away, his face set in harsh lines as he hunkered over her, his knee moving between her thighs and spreading them before he drove inside her. "Soon, I'll become little more than memory to you."

Tyriel screamed in ecstasy as Jaren slammed into her from behind, his long hands gripping her hips and holding her still as his cock tunneled through her wet, swollen depths.

The shield of silence they had placed around the room also contained the wild magick that was breaking free. Rainbows broke over her skin and she sobbed out his name as he pounded into her, groaning her name and digging his nails into her hips.

One long, muscled forearm jerked her up, pinning her slim body against his longer, powerful one and his other hand speared through the small, neatly trimmed nest of curls between her thighs. His fingers caught her clit, pinching it, and she flew off into climax with a sob as he sank his teeth into her shoulder and pummeled her, his cock jerking as he pumped her full of his seed.

She was sighing with bliss as he rolled them onto their sides and cuddled her against him.

"Are you staying?" he murmured in elvish, stroking her damp hair from her neck and kissing it.

"Lower the shield so that I can hear when the humans wake," she muttered, reaching up and linking her hand with his. "I'll stay 'til dawn."

He slid his knee between hers. "Then I'll lower the shield later. I'm not done making you scream yet."

He saw her leaving Jaren's room as he left theirs. Her hair was sexily tossed and tangled from sleep and sex, her mouth swollen and red from the night's pleasure. A faint red mark marred the golden perfection of her neck and her white shift was gone, replaced by a laced man's shirt that barely hid the shadow of her nipples.

Jealousy, red and ugly, raced through Aryn and he clamped it down.

Not for me—she isn't for me, he reminded himself as she sleepily rubbed her eyes, looking innocent and sexy and so damned sweet as she leaned back against the door, still half asleep, and totally unaware he watched her.

"There's people about," he said softly.

Her lids lifted slowly and she smiled sleepily at him. "G'mornin," she mumbled as she padded toward him, yawning.

He could smell her, sweet, always so damn sweet, but now there was another scent on her, the scent of another man's body, sweat and seed clinging to her. Aryn clenched his jaw as she passed by him, her soft curls grazing his arm.

All he wanted, all, was to push her into the room and erase that scent and replace it with his own. His cock throbbed, blood pounding heavily within it as the image of doing just that haunted him, augmented by Irian's damnable magick as the enchanter roused and caught a hint of Aryn's need. She would be wet, swollen, her pussy full of her cream and another man's seed. And after Aryn had filled her full of his own, he'd bathe her clean and then taste her—he'd been aching for just one taste.

"Then do it. Taste her, fuck her, love her."

121

The door closed behind Tyriel as Irian murmured encouragement into his mind.

With a snarl, Aryn stomped down the stairs, away from temptation.

"Ye want her. Take her. She'll welcome ye wi' open arms."

Aryn flung up a wall against Irian's compelling voice, grabbing the axe from the wall and heading for the pile of wood. His hands closed convulsively around the wooden handle, sweat covering his body in the cool morning air.

Bloody hell.

* * * * *

Aryn was drawn outside two days later. It was nearing sunset. Moon dark was tomorrow. Tyriel was busily serving food, but she had talked Jaren into playing his flute for the crowd.

The elf had not been happy about it either.

Aryn wasn't happy about a number of things, namely the fact that she had not slept in their room once since the elf had arrived. It bothered him and there was no reason for it.

Irian's husky chuckle echoed in the back of his mind. *"Are ye truly so blind, Aryn of Olsted? Have I an imbecile wielding me?"* the enchanter asked dryly as Aryn left the warmth of the tavern for the cool night air.

"Must you speak in riddles so much?" Aryn asked nastily.

"*'Tis simple enough, if you opened your bloody fool eyes,*" Irian responded as Aryn propped his back against the wall.

And froze.

Irian felt it as well.

Blackness...

"*It searches for an offering,*" Irian growled menacingly. "*Tyriel did not make herself known to it. It looks for a weaker, more visible target.*"

Aryn moved to shove off the wall. And found he was frozen. "I thought we'd agreed you'd not be taking over my body anymore," he growled out.

"*Aye, that we did. But if ye go plunging neck deep into yer death, the elf willna be forgiving me,*" Irian said coolly. "*We wait for her and the cold one.*"

"I've been fighting without her a bloody long time," Aryn hissed.

"*But not anything like this,*" Irian said with certainty. "*If I canna take over yer body, then I can only work so much enchantment. And you've no magick to call your own yet. We wait.*"

But they didn't have to wait long.

Jaren appeared first, moving out of the shadows like he was one of them, his dark, gleaming eyes assessing Aryn without a blink, without a word as he waited for Tyriel. Irian released his hold once the dark elf appeared, saying on a sigh, *"You will wait for the Jiupsu, Aryn. You'd hate for that one t' have t' take ye down."*

Aryn growled out a vile curse and wished again the bloody enchanter could take form so he could knock him down. At least once. Irian chuckled. *"Until the scales are balanced, the sword is the form I have, unless I take yours,"* he added with a shrug as his misty body shimmered into view.

The question, "What scales…" faded from his mind as Tyriel landed between them on the balls of her feet, clad not in her serving girl's skirt, but in black leather like the other elf wore, her hair woven into a tight braid, her own blade lying snug in its sheath down her back, her amber eyes glinting. "It's time?" she asked quietly.

"Something pulls us," Aryn said, unable to explain beyond that.

It was enough. She waited for Aryn to take the lead and then she followed him.

Jaren fell into step behind her, his long cloak fluttering around his ankles as he moved soundlessly. Aryn's hearing was sharp, especially for a human's, but while on occasion he could hear Tyriel's light footfalls, if he hadn't looked back from time to time and seen him, he would not have known Jaren was there.

"A deadly one, that," Irian murmured as Aryn met the elf's eyes in the dim light and they took the final corner before the street opened up to the Inferno—the neighborhood where the Whore's Guild had chosen to set up their trade. The elf's mouth curled up slightly at one corner as he caught Aryn's eye, but then he broke contact and stood studying the buildings before them.

"For this, you have left the Fair Kingdoms," he mused to Tyriel in an even voice.

"No. Not for this," she said, shaking her head. "For freedom. And in the Fair Kingdoms, there are many who think that this is all I would be good for." Then she stepped forward, lifting her face to the dark sky, her hands open, palms outward. "They've not gotten started just yet—no blood has been spilled. We have a little time."

She studied the ground and a smile curved her lips when she found what she was seeking. Aryn saw it as well and sighed. Into the tunnels below the city they were going. Jaren closed his eyes briefly and said, "If I were not loyal to you, Princess—"

"I'm no Princess any longer," she said easily, taking the iron cross-gate cover in her hands and lifting it easily before either man reached her side to do it. "I left my father's side and his home, his lands and the title he tried to secure for me. You need not come with me if you do not choose, Jaren."

He continued as if she hadn't spoken. "If I were not loyal to you, Princess, and your father, I believe I would strangle you for even thinking I would follow you in that cesspit. Perhaps my loyalty is misplaced. Perhaps I should take you back—"

She slid him a cocky glance and said, "Perhaps you should try living in the real world instead of the Fair Kingdoms, Jaren." And then she leaped lightly down into the dark maw, landing on her feet and as Aryn jumped down behind her, she held out one hand. In it, a ball of white light formed to light their way. It softened to a golden yellow as Jaren came down behind them.

Aryn said, "Someone may see to the cover —"

But Jaren had lifted one hand, and as Aryn spoke the cover was floating gently down to settle over the hole, covering their passing as if it hadn't happened. Jaren was staring around him, eyeing a rat as he blandly said, "The real world. If this is the real world, 'tis glad I am that I live in the Fair Kingdoms, Princess." He'd paid no attention as the cover had settled over the hole, blocking off the dim light from above.

Tyriel ignored him and beckoned to Aryn. Aryn moved closer to her and Jaren fell in step behind him. "Can Irian protect you against most magick?" she asked as they started down the narrow passage. "He protected you against the sorcery that night, but what about elemental magery? Enchantment?"

Aryn felt the soft rustle in his mind as Irian moved out of his 'resting place' and then the enchanter shimmered into view, laughing softly. *"I am an enchanter, lady of the Jiupsu. A sorry one I would be if I could not protect him against enchantment. But I would have to borrow his body and blood for a time."*

"A time?" Tyriel and Aryn asked in unison, doubtfully. Jaren studied him with curious eyes.

Irian laughed, a deep, husky laugh that filled the tunnel and made both Aryn and Tyriel shiver. Jaren just continued to stare at the enchanter. *"A time, a few moments. Long enough to draw blood and raise wards,"* he said, smiling slowly at Aryn's obvious discomfort. *"'Tis a sad day when I must beg permission to protect my ward, Aryn."*

Aryn asked grudgingly, "What must I do?"

Irian moved closer and Aryn felt the enchanter settle inside him, but not taking him over, more like he was sliding inside his skin with Aryn."*Watch…learn…remember,*" Irian purred inside his head. "*First, we draw the blade. His name was Asrel. Once. Long ago. Much magick had to be forged into him to make him withstand the ages. He belonged to my father –* "

Images swirled inside Aryn's head as he drew the blade—the land much more primitive, wilder, newer, a man, similar to Irian forging a blade, breathing magick and life and blood into the blade as he shaped the enchanted iron while a wide-eyed youth looked on from the safety of the yard.

Blood, death, mayhem, a young girl's scream, the father's sightless eyes, a woman, Irian's mother, somehow Aryn knew, who lay dead, her body raped and battered and mutilated before they granted her death. And the youth, not even fifteen, taking up the sword.

"*Asrel.*" Irian whispered the blade's name as Aryn whirled the blade in front of him, almost hypnotized, remembering. No, reliving Irian's memories. "*We must place our palm along the blade's edge, my brother, but we canna cut too deep. Do not be worrying, though, Asrel will heal the wound. He always has before.*" And Aryn remembered that he had done this before, with Irian controlling him, and then blocking the memories.

Aryn barely felt the sharp metal slice through the toughened flesh of his palm and he stared at the welling blood for a long moment before Irian guided him into sheathing the blade with his uninjured hand and smearing his index finger through the blood. "*If we were protecting the ground we watched, it would be a circle we paced. But we ward ourselves. Gather earth, spit, and salt."*

"I don't carry salt," Aryn said. His voice sounded loud. Too loud.

Irian laughed. *"Aye, but you do. Look in your belt, my brother. What kind of —"*

"...Enchanter would you be if you let your ward go out without salt," Aryn finished in a mumble as he reached into his belt and rifled through it. And lo and behold, a small vial of salt. Fine-grained, and worth a small fortune. Cupping his bleeding fist to keep the blood from spilling, he added the salt, the earth and then spat into his hand, listening to Irian's voice and making the paste with a curl of his lip. He dimly heard Tyriel laugh. "The fastidious enchanter," she murmured to Jaren. "Oh, wouldn't he hate earth witchery?"

He was also distantly aware of Irian's amused chuckle but he was too focused on the heat in his soul, something he hadn't ever felt before. *"That's the magick, boy. It's becoming a part of you...the more we do together, the more it becomes a part of you,"* Irian said softly. Aryn felt Irian settle more firmly inside his body and realized he was just a watcher now as Irian's magick took over. *"Not mine...ours...and soon...it will be yours."*

Symbols etched onto Aryn's face, wrists and hands. One on his chest. Irian's deep, guttural voice echoed out of Aryn's mouth and foreign words filled the tunnel as the runes on Aryn's skin started to seep into his body. The heat started to spread outward and took on color and form, a silvery blue in the corner of Aryn's eyes that disappeared every time he tried to turn and focus on it.

"The ward. And you can see it. Enchantment takes its hold on you, more and more," Irian mused as he left Aryn's body with a sigh and shimmered back into view. He bowed to Tyriel and said, *"He is protected against any magick that may be thrown at him — save for mind magick. The protection from mind magick has always come from the blade. Asrel's magick still holds, after all these years. A fine blade, like none other in the world. Only the Jiupsu could have forged such a blade of steel and magick and have it hold after all this time."*

Jaren turned to look at them, his dark-green eyes gleaming against his pale skin. "We must go — something calls to me," he murmured. "A child, suffering and screaming." He started to run lightly down the tunnel, his feet flying soundlessly over the dirt, so fast Aryn could not keep pace with him.

Tyriel followed, swearing under her breath and Aryn took up the rear, casting one glance at what little he could see of the sky through the grid of the iron cover. He quickly lost sight of the elves but continued to run, trusting his night vision and the ghostly glow of Irian at his side. *"Something is amiss, brother. I feel much anger, much hatred."*

When he barreled around the corner, he saw Tyriel bracing Jaren away from the wall, her chin up and her eyes narrowed as she arrogantly said, "As your Princess, I command you to step down."

"Then I renounce my —"

"Mecaro! Esiyencio!" she rasped, gesturing with one hand toward him and the taller elf's eyes narrowed as he opened his mouth but no sound came out. He started to lift a hand but froze. *"Ceano mora fovan."*

"High Elvish hasna changed much — silence, still your tongue. Do not move," Irian translated with a smile. *"An odd package, this gypsy-elf. Not just an elemental mage, like she tried to tell me. She bespelled him well and truly."*

But Aryn heard little the enchanter said.

"Do you think I cannot feel her crying out?" Tyriel said, her eyes gleaming with tears, her voice husky and deep. "There is a girl with fae blood in there, aye, I feel it. But more, there is a child in there, innocent and hurting, but rushing in there blindly will only get her killed, Jaren. You are De Asir, one of the legendary assassins of the Fair Kingdoms, a vengeance killer. You know this. Think with your head, not your heart. That is what she needs."

Then she merely blinked and Jaren swore, his hand snapping out, grabbing her neck. He whirled and pinned her against the wall quicker than Aryn's eyes could track, but he had already drawn his sword, unaware he had even moved until his blade was at Jaren's neck, before Jaren had so much as opened his mouth.

"Be at ease, Aryn," Tyriel said, smiling slightly. "He means me no harm."

Without even glancing at Aryn, Jaren whispered savagely, "If you were not right, I would kill you for what you might have cost her." Then he released her and stepped back, his eyes never leaving Tyriel's face. "Every second we wait takes her closer to things worse than death."

She smiled, once, sadly. And then she drew a small blade and pierced her flesh. *"Viastra..."*

The earth parted and a small orb floated up, revealing a teenaged girl with wild, frightened eyes and a circle of men who paid as much attention to her as they would to a pig trussed over a fire. "*Viearne*," Tyriel whispered, turning to look at the wall.

The earth started to move and part.

"The lights will dim. Aryn, you will have to let Irian in enough so that he may guide your movements a little. We must move fast. They have cut her and she bleeds. Badly, she bleeds. I can smell it, feel it, the earth reeks with it. She needs healing," Tyriel said quietly. Her body trembled minutely and her eyes fluttered closed for a brief second.

As the wall of earth that separated them thinned down to the manmade barrier, Tyriel indicated in trader's sign that they be silent, though all knew. Then she whispered, "*Kebasti*."

An explosion shook the ground, for miles around it seemed. They rushed in as the lights went out, the fire died and everything went black. Men shouted and hurled questions but didn't realize it was an attack as Aryn felt Irian settle behind his eyes like a hand inside a glove. A man stumbled into him and set up the alarm. Sword drawn, Aryn took him down and turned to face another, snarling as he smelled the blood staining this man's robe.

Someone was chanting and Jaren shouted out Tyriel's name as he tried to mark her location in the darkness. Moving, searching by instinct alone, he found the girl, and clasped her to his chest. Protecting her with his body, he spun her away from the danger. Irian started to speak through Aryn's mouth but Tyriel said quietly, commandingly, "This one is mine, enchanter."

A man lit a fire and light came back into the room as Aryn turned to face two men rushing blindly at him. He snarled at them tauntingly and laughed when the magicks they flung at him hit his ward and dissolved. Another man reached for him with a hand that glowed and swirled. A ghostly hand reached out of the mists and grabbed the man's hand and that hand turned gray, and withered, spreading up his arm, until his entire body was encompassed by it and he fell to the floor dead.

Tyriel smiled slowly, coldly, moving in on the man who had started to chant. "*Mecaro*, you perverted, evil wretched thing. *Esiyencio*, before I cut your tongue out myself," she purred, placing one foot in front of the other as she advanced on him, drawing the long slim blade at her waist. His eyes widened as she faced him and let him see, truly see what she was. "Oh, but it has been a long time since I have had the pleasure of dealing with scum such as you."

The man's blood-red hair whipped back from his face as an unseen wind filled the chamber. His hands moved, almost elf-quick, and a cut appeared on Tyriel's face. She gasped and pressed the back of her hand against it. "Now that wasn't very nice," she said, studying the blood that stained her hand. It trickled down her cheek, her neck, as she moved closer. "*Ceano mora fovan.*"

And as Jaren had done, the man went stock-still, frozen in place as Tyriel paced a long, slow circle around him. "Now, what to do with you? Send you to the Soulless Planes? The demons there so love to feast on the flesh of the living. Perhaps we could let the—"

Something knocked her down, unseen, unfelt, but there all the same. A black, stinking evil filled the room, and Tyriel's eyes narrowed as she climbed to her feet. "Bad, bad little mortal...calling up a demon, don't you know what they can do to you if they don't catch their prey? You become the prey." Turning, she tried to track the new creature that had let itself into the chamber.

"I do not fear the darkness," she whispered as the amber moonstone at her neck started to gleam. But the moonstone's gleaming paled in comparison to the glowing from the pendant next to it. The crucifix glowed as though it had taken the moon within it, silvery white, lighting up the chamber and casting a glow onto the man in front of her as she said, "I have nothing to fear from you. Show yourself."

She felt the amusement coming from the man who was held, still and silent, by her bonds. Smiling, she felt his amusement turn into dismay and shock as her order was obeyed. "Demons feed on fear. Their power comes from it. Their illusions stem from it—he is not truly invisible, on this plane, or any other. Not since you summoned him here. I do not fear him and that steals his power."

The shape forming in front of her was hardly a frightening one. It was a gleaming white spear of ivory beauty. Until she looked into its eyes and saw the very fires of hell gleaming there. "Leave me to the master, magicked one, and I will not harm you," it rasped, turning its angry eyes to the man who had summoned it.

Tyriel shook her head. "As much as we'd like to, that cannot happen. He deserves the death you would mete him, but then you would not be bound to him or any place or thing. And what creature, mortal or fae, deserves that, other than him and his ilk?"

"It is not your fight, go now." The gleaming demon turned away.

She studied his horned head, the spiked shoulders, his long, oddly slender form so stretched and out of proportion. Her eyes closed and she remembered. "*Mevitecaz.*"

The demon froze.

"*Mevitecaz.*"

He whirled to face her with a roar and lunged for her. Throwing up her hands, she braced herself just as the ward formed and he struck it. "The elvin kin hold the Book of Demons. We all must know it. I know who you are and why you were banished from the Fifth Plane. Shall I send you to an even lower level of hell?"

Aryn moved to rush forward.

Jaren caught his arm and smiled thinly. He still held the girl cradled against his chest.

"Just watch. And wait."

It was hours after dawn and Aryn had still not slept.

Tyriel lay pale, near lifeless on the bed. Jaren had assured him she was merely drained. She hadn't killed the demon—she had indeed banished it to the lowest level in hell and it had gone fighting and cursing her name and striking out at her.

She bore a mark from it—a long silvery slash that had torn across her breast, slicing through her clothing, and marking her. There was bruising around it, but the mark itself was silver and felt hot to the touch. Aryn had touched it while cleaning it and it had left a burn on his hand that had blistered. It crossed from her right shoulder down her breast, just below the nipple and on down her torso, wrapping under and around her side.

"It will heal, but scar." Jaren stood at the foot of the bed.

"How did you get in here?" Aryn asked wearily. The door bloody well did not open.

Jaren smiled slightly. "She is strong. This weakened her, but she will be fit and whole within a few weeks," he said. "But how much of the night she remembers, I do not know. The heat of a demon battle sometimes takes on a strange quality. We oft times forget them, in pieces, or in whole. But the mark may remind her. The one who summoned the demon escaped, but the others are dead. I would hunt him but I must get the child to Averne."

"Tyriel—"

"She needs you at her side," Jaren said coolly, lifting a black brow. "She will not go back to Averne. If I send back warriors to bring her, she will level them with a blink. But she cannot be alone. If by chance I encounter her mother's people, I will send them."

"I was not about to leave her alone, but the man cannot be allowed to get away," Aryn snarled.

Jaren's eyes gleamed red around the edges. "Neither man nor beast can hide from De Asir. I have his scent, his name, his magick. I will hunt him, I will find him. But not now," Jaren said softly. His eyes, his thoughts drifted down the hall to the sleeping girl on his bed. "Now I have a wounded soul I must take to my people."

"Your people threw out a wounded soul because her mother was gypsy. Why will they care for that one?"

Jaren laughed. "Because Tyriel wasn't broken," he said softly. "There is nothing that makes the kin feel more needed than the need to fix the downtrodden and the broken. But I am not taking her there for them to fix. I am taking her there for my lord and lady. If my sister Aradelle cannot heal her body, and Averne cannot heal her soul, nothing can."

Aryn lowered his head to study Tyriel's face and he smiled. "No, Tyriel is definitely not broken—"

But he was talking to himself.

The room was empty.

Jaren lifted the heavily drugged woman-child in his arms, his heart bleeding, rage eating at him. They had tried to destroy this lovely thing. Nearly had. *Your days are numbered, blood mage. Know that…and think of me while you sleep.* Psychic skills were a rare talent among the kin, and powerful ones were even rarer.

And when he felt the man's fear, Jaren smiled coldly as he carried his precious burden out into the silent streets.

His elvish stallion was waiting outside the city walls. A ride that would take an average horse a week could have them at Averne in two days. Which was why Jaren had her so heavily drugged—he didn't want her to wake until he had her in Averne. The ride would take its toll in pain.

And for every whimper he heard as they rode, he filed it away, stored it, remembered it.

For the time would come...

Chapter Eight
Five years later

Irian was pulling at him.

Tyriel could see the strain in his eyes, almost hear the internal fight.

She slid the sword a withering glance and thought silently, *"What do you want now, blasted enchanter?"*

"You." He flooded her mind with images of them, nude on brightly colored silk sheets, in the tents favored by her gypsy blood.

She blushed to the roots of her hair and turned her head away so that Aryn didn't catch sight of her reddened face and wonder why. Irian had shielded his thoughts from his bearer, the way he always did when thinking of Tyriel in an earthier sense. *"The man is a bloody fool, he is,"* Irian murmured into her mind. An unseen hand seemed to stroke down the back of her head, along her thick braid and down her back to rest above the curve of her ass.

"I thought when ye took up arms together as partners he would take your bed as well, but 'tis pure madness. And he torments me w' his talk of not bedding a swordmate. Bah! Five long years has he resisted…how much longer must we wait?"

She suppressed a shiver as those final words seemed to be whispered right into her ear. *"Would you leave me be?"*

"But you are so much easier t' torment," Irian purred. "Warm, female, sweet. I'd rather be sinking into your sweet little cleft, but your mind is almost as sweet."

"And is this why you torment your bearer? You insist on fucking me?"

"Nay," Irian's voice grew strained. "You know me better, wild elf, pretty Jiupsu. I canna stand the thought of goin' to Ifteril. Something is there. Something evil, something dark, something that threatens us. But Aryn says we winter there. Contracts. Fucking contracts."

"We've signed no contracts to fuck," Tyriel answered absently. She didn't like it. Never had the enchanter balked at the thought of going anywhere. Something evil...something dark. A shiver took her body and she absently touched her fingers to the chains that hung between her breasts.

"I fear for you, elf." Irian's voice came to her on a gruff whisper and his presence folded around her like a cloak, safe, protective.

And Aryn rode on, oblivious.

The blasted enchanter was talking to Tyriel again.

Aryn could hear the throaty rumble in the back of his mind but the words were unclear.

Whatever Irian was saying was disturbing Tyriel. And it disturbed her clear into the night.

Her smooth dusky skin had gone pale, and her face was tight with strain. Her normally smooth, subtle movements were awkward as they set up camp that night.

Lowering herself beside the fire, her eyes were haunted, dark, sightless, as she stared into nothingness. She tucked her glossy black ringlets behind her ears, the elongated point holding the wild curls away when a human's ears would have done nothing. The left ear had a golden ring pierced through, halfway through the top, and a cuff that hugged her lobe, the gold reflecting the firelight as she sat staring somberly into space.

"What bothers you?" he asked quietly.

She lifted her eyes from the fire and stared at him, slowly, almost as if she were drugged, or entranced. "Irian doesn't want to go into to Ifteril." Her tongue slid out past her lips, wetted them, and Aryn suppressed a ragged groan as her eyes closed again.

Fuck, we've got to get to Ifteril, into a city, before I lose it. For five years, he had managed to keep a hold on his craving for her, but long treks like this, between cities, when there were no women around to ride and pretend it was her underneath him — it drove him mad.

"We signed a contract, Tyriel." His words were strained but she seemed not to notice.

"I do not want to go. The enchanter's words bothered me. Greatly. Something dark...something evil," she whispered, her lashes lifting slowly, revealing her amber eyes, glowing, reflecting the firelight, gleaming like the stone that swung between her breasts. Above it, the crucifix gleamed silver, winking at him, reminding him of the mark that marred the smooth perfection of her skin under clothes, the demon's mark that she had received five years ago in battle. "Contract be damned, something deadly waits for us in Ifteril."

She was hiding something. It was there in her eyes.

"What aren't you telling me?" he asked quietly.

Her lashes lowered. "Nothing. I just do not wish to go. We can winter elsewhere. Anywhere. With the caravans again, or even in Averne. I dare say my cousins could drum up a dozen good substitutes for us, and a dozen good reasons why we cannot go."

"Does our word mean nothing, then?" he asked softly. "Tell me why. You know more than you are saying, elf. What waits in Ifteril?"

Tyriel's shoulders slumped. She shifted and lay down, rolling onto her side, away from the fire. "Very well. We go to Ifteril."

"Danger and darkness wait, and all for her."

Aryn rose from his bedroll, unable to sleep. He was pacing far away from camp to avoid disturbing his partner, and of course, the blasted enchanter couldn't leave him be.

Turning, he met the eyes of the long-dead enchanter as he wavered into view. "Tyriel is in danger?" he asked doubtfully. "She can handle any blasted thing that comes her way."

"Not this time. Turn back, before she is lost to you."

"Why do you insist on talking like the woman belongs to me?" Aryn growled, advancing on Irian. "She is not mine. Not ours."

"She could be yours. Take her. Keep her, love her."

"Love her? Her? Keep her?" Aryn sputtered, unaware that Tyriel had risen from her bedroll and stood in the distance, listening.

"Aye. The girl loves you madly. The need is an ache in her belly to be with you, feel you."

"You'd tell me any damn thing it took if you thought it would get me to climb atop her and fuck her," Aryn growled, his hands closing into fists as he fought the urge to do just that. "She is not for me. I am not for her. We are partners, nothing more. We will never be more."

"You deny that she is in your heart. You will admit you want her, because wanting a woman is easy," Irian said softly. His long curling hair shifted around his shoulders as he moved closer to Aryn, his golden skin gleaming in the black night. His widely spaced dark eyes narrowed and he smiled slowly. *"You want to touch her, taste her, fuck her...love her. Do it."*

"No. If I need a woman, want a woman, I'll find a fucking whore in Ifteril," Aryn snapped, glaring at Irian with furious eyes, his body rigid and aching with hunger. His cock throbbed against his belly and all he wanted, all, was lying in her bedroll, not far away. *Yes! All I want lies there. All.* But he kept the words locked behind his teeth. "But I am not fucking Tyriel just to please a dead enchanter."

"And what about to please her? Yourself?"

"I can please myself with my fist."

Her eyes stinging with tears, Tyriel backed away in silence, her belly hot and tight with grief. She made sure to muffle her presence, physically, magickally. Aryn and Irian couldn't know she had been there.

And she was leaving.

She could avoid whatever danger lurked in Ifteril long enough to gather supplies. And then she'd go home.

To Averne.

Aryn awoke the next morning to a cold, silent camp.

That alone told him something was terribly wrong.

Tyriel never slept longer than he did. An elvish warrior needed so little sleep. She was always awake before him, always had the fire built back up, breakfast ready, the camp broken down as she walked around humming under her breath.

"The elf isna here."

Aryn looked up to see Irian's form striding into camp. "I can see that, you blasted hunk of tin."

"She heard you last night, saw us talking."

Aryn's mouth dropped open. "And you didn't say anything?" he rasped, rising off his bedroll, chest bare, hands clenched. *If, by some slim chance, the enchanter was right, and she had heard him...* "What in the blasted hells were you thinking?"

"I didna know she was there. I knew only after I worked enchantment. Watch, see." Aryn felt his hand lifted even though he wasn't the one lifting it. He drew his blade without realizing it and pierced his flesh—and saw the ball of smoke rising from the ground. He knew it, easily, and could do it of his own free will now. Irian's enchantment was taking root in Aryn. The magick was settling in Aryn's bones and blood and he could do, easily

and quickly, simple, small enchantments, with no help or guidance.

But Irian's displeasure had him taking Aryn over, a sure and certain sign of just how fucking mad the enchanter was. And Aryn saw why as the smoke cleared, revealing Tyriel as her sleepy eyes opened. She slid from her bedroll, stretching, the camisole riding up and revealing a slim, toned belly, naked and appealing. Her hands slid unconsciously up her torso before she slid them through her tumbled curls and absently rubbed her eyes before looking around for something.

Someone.

Aryn knew when she spotted them. A soft, sad little smile appeared on her face.

And he knew the enchanter had been right.

She moved closer, in total silence, and he could sense the magick that flowed from her, and her automatic muffling of it, which is why Irian didn't sense her. And Aryn had to watch as tears filled her eyes, as she heard his words and staggered from them.

"Bloody blasted, cruel bastard."

Aryn turned and stared at Irian.

"Where is she?"

"I know not. I am not omnipotent. And Tyriel is not my bearer. I know not her heart and mind, other than what she tells me and what I can see for myself. But I suspect she has gone into Ifteril."

Alone.

Her supplies would have to wait until she had money. She left Kilidare untethered outside the towne walls since Bel wasn't there to keep him company and the elvish stallion took off at a wild gallop. With a stern thought, she told him, *Be ready. We are not staying long.*

Ready. Ready. Promise.

Painting a bold as brass smile on her face, she made her way through the crowded streets, unaware that she had caught the eye of somebody who knew her face, her magick. If she hadn't been shielding so tightly against Irian, she would have sensed him.

His dark eyes roamed over her face, his blood-red braid pulled back and tucked down under his shirt. His hood kept him in shadow. He made note of the inn she stopped in, and waited. She didn't come out.

Tainan Delre smiled slowly, coldly. She had walked right to him. The little bitch who had taken his power circle five years ago had walked right to him. And without the tall, warrior men at her side. Oh, aye, she had battled the demon and won. But it was the dark-haired elf that had truly frightened Tainan. A snarl spread across his face—frightened. That she had led something into his life that still sickened him, that still caused him sleepless nights…oh, she would pay for that. That she had led somebody into his world who had caused him fear—that anything had caused him fear—was something unforgivable. She would pay with blood, sex, fear, magick and death—and she would pay so slowly.

All it would take was her blood, her magick, and he would be restored to what he had once been.

What he had been before that battle five years ago.

Then he could start again, anew, but he would be more careful. No cities this time. Only his homeland, and he would pluck stragglers, or lone women traveling. Even couples, and kill the man as he raped the woman—that fear and anger would be a bonus.

Soon... he could have it all again soon.

And all because she had wandered into this town. The blood of an elvish warrior was a fine pure rush, and such a sacrifice she would be, once broken.

The scar marring the right side of his face twisted as he smiled. Walking away from the inn, he felt lighter, filled with purpose. He would return, tonight. And he would take her.

Irian homed in on Tyriel like a beacon, finding the inn where she had lit within an hour of entering the crowded, dark city of Ifteril. Aryn could have searched for hours, days, or weeks, and perhaps never have seen her.

The enchanter found her easily, quickly.

And furiously.

"The lass bloody well knows she is in danger...I warned her foolish hide—she doesna listen t'reason."

Aryn stood in the shadow, listening to her play. She had donned one of her few gypsy garbs, a brightly colored, low-cut red blouse, with a corselet that laced over it, a full skirt, her hair flowing wild and free down her back. Looking for money, and fast. "I don't think she is much in the way of reasoning right now, but Tyriel isn't helpless."

"Tyriel isn't thinking right now, you fucking fool," Irian snarled at him. He shimmered into view. It no longer

worried Aryn that others would see him. Irian could allow others to see him, if he chose, but only by his choosing was he seen. *"There is somethin' black, hideous after her and she needs t' be thinkin' but she isna thinkin' a'tall."*

She was so lovely, so ethereal, and so earthy at the same time. With the blood of the elves and the gypsies in her, how could she be otherwise? *"Go to her."* Irian's urging was bone-deep, blood boiling urgent. That Aryn wanted to so badly was all the more reason to resist. *"She is safe, so long as she is by your side."*

"So now I fuck her to keep her safe?"

The lively music of the flute skipped a beat, and Aryn swore, his eyes flying across the room, meeting hers, those dark, deep eyes. She had heard him. Again. Over the music, the laugher, the shouts, those damnable exotic, elvin ears had heard the one thing he had said out loud, the one thing that sounded so damn cruel.

Her lids lowered and the music played on.

She had known the minute they came through the door. Irian's presence, his overwhelming rage and relief crashed into her mind, and she couldn't help but feel relieved herself. Darkness had eaten at her almost all day, but she wasn't sure if it was her own pain, or something more.

Aryn's eyes had roamed over her, like a hand, firm and strong, almost palpable in its intensity. Her nipples were still peaked, pressed hard against her silk blouse, the gay colors of her clan bringing false color to her skin. Under the long skirt, she shifted her legs, crossed them, the leather of her thigh-high boots hugging her legs. She was wet, weeping with want for him, and his words rang once more in her ears. *So now I fuck her to keep her safe?*

She hardened her heart and willed magick into her playing, uncaring that it was morally wrong. She wanted, needed that money. She was leaving in the morning, and going home to Averne.

"Stop playing."

She ignored his low voice. And played.

A dark shadow came through the door and her eyes landed on him as a cold sinking fear slid through her belly. There lies death. The man, tall, cloaked and silent, settled in a corner watching her. Tearing her eyes from him, and her concentration from Aryn, she played.

Some time had passed. Aryn had gotten his own room, her sharp hearing told her, a large comfortable, clean one, the best the inn had to offer, and after that he had accepted some ale and food from the passing barmaid. She had offered him a bit more as well, and Tyriel wondered sourly why in hell Aryn had told this one no.

Shoving it out of her mind, she let her eyes wander back to the man in black, whose eyes and face she couldn't see.

"Tyriel."

She stared at the man in the long black cloak and played as a hand, hard, firm, familiar came up to rest on her neck, oddly possessive and warm. As his skin touched hers, the black, terrified feeling in her belly lightened and died away. Something inside her whispered, *Forget your pride, your heart. Stay with him...* Part of her knew that once she left him, she was no longer safe from whatever blackness Irian had foretold.

Blackness seemed to linger around the man who had settled in a corner, staring at her.

With malevolence and malice.

Aryn lowered his head and whispered into her ear, brushing aside her curls, "Stop playing, now, or I'll carry your fine little ass out of here." He squeezed her neck in warning as he spoke then stepped back and studied her, waiting.

She finished the song with a flourish and stooped to gather her money. With a quick, expert eye, she figured the money would buy the basic supplies she needed and then some. And she could always do some busking to earn a little extra. Scooping it into her pouch, she stowed her flute, but before she could toss her pack over her shoulder, Aryn had taken it and moved through the small door to the side that led to the rooms.

"What?" she demanded coldly, folding her arms over her chest and staring at him, refusing to relinquish the flute or her smaller travel pack when he reached for them after closing the door behind them.

She heard Irian...not his words...just a murmuring, in the back of her mind. With a snarl, she said, "Stay out of this, you bloody, blasted enchanter."

Aryn lifted his eyes to her face, those dark, dreamy blue eyes that had totally captured her heart almost from the first. Irian shimmered into view and stared at Tyriel as well, his intense, hungry gaze rapt on her face. *"You canna understand, Tyriel, love. You didna hear all —"*

"Fuck it. And fuck you both."

Aryn whispered quietly, "That's the whole problem. That's what we both want. But I am not going to condemn myself to pining after a gypsy-elf who will be forever young and lovely while I will soon fade away. I am mortal, just a man. You are not, you have the blood of divine beings in your veins."

Tyriel felt her mouth tremble as she stared into Aryn's eyes and saw an answering heat there. But it was only heat. Only heat, not love nor need. "You have never been just a man, Aryn of Olsted. But I will not stay here any longer. And we both know neither you nor Irian can force me." She turned her back and headed for the door, uncaring that she didn't have her other pack, just needing to leave.

"She canna go…I am sorry for breaking my word."

Aryn opened his mouth, unaware of what Irian was talking about, and not really caring. He wasn't letting her walk out that door.

But he never said a word, never remembered anything beyond the sight of her slim back covered in black leather, all those wilds curls spilling down to rest just above her ass, the gay red of her sleeves moving in a silken whisper as she turned one last time to glance at him, her eyes glowing luminously.

And then Irian swarmed up and overwhelmed.

Tyriel glimpsed Aryn in those eyes, grim, determined. But then his eyes went blank. And then hungry, sorry, dark...Irian...

"Does your word mean so little?" she asked softly.

"You mean more." His voice was deeper, slower, gruffer than Aryn's, his eyes hotter, heavier. "You canna leave us, him. You are safe with him. You will stay."

"Irian, *nebaste*..." she whispered, half-heartedly as he backed her up against the door. "Stop...please...this solves nothing. You are not Aryn. I am not in love with you."

"But part of you wants me almost as much as you want him." Irian aligned Aryn's long, rangy powerful body against hers, his thick, throbbing cock fitting into the notch between her thighs. "Ye canna deny me that, girl...can ye?"

Tyriel's words died in a moan as his hands fisted in her hair and arched her face up, his tongue pushed between her lips, bringing Aryn's taste, his scent, but something darker, and different, something more primitive, wilder. Irian.

He rasped, "You will scream my name this night...before this night ends, I will hear it, I swear you that." Tyriel wasn't so certain that he was wrong. His hands, hard and callused, grasped the sleeves of her silken blouse and she gasped into his mouth as she felt him tear it away. Then from under the form-fitting leather corselet, until the silken blouse was lying in shreds at her feet and she wore only the leather corselet and her skirt and boots as Irian moved away, holding her back, one hand at her neck, the other at her hip. "*Jiupsu...aakin su rrieul Jiupsu...*" he crooned, staring at her.

Disconcerting, it was, hearing ancient, archaic gypsy flowing from Aryn's mouth, especially as her vision started to waver and Irian's image kept trying to superimpose itself over Aryn's body. "Lovely lady of the Jiupsu." His hands gripped her skirt and he pushed it down over her hips until she stood naked in front of him, save for her boots and the corselet, her cheeks flushing pink as he stared up at her, his dark eyes heating with an inner flame that turned Tyriel's blood into lava.

Cream started to pool inside her cleft, and her heart started to beat with slow, pounding throbs. Irian's nostrils flared and he scented her, his lips parting. His eyes focused on her body, clad in the corselet that rose to just under her breasts, pushing them up, two thin straps trailing up over her shoulders, and down her back. In front, the laces were pulled tight, revealing an inch of tanned toned flesh and Irian lifted his eyes to study her breasts so prominently displayed, nipples drawn tight and puckered, waist cinched down by the gleaming black leather. The corselet arrowed down to the hair that covered the mound of her sex, and the black boots that came up over her knees, elvish boots, form-fitting, tight, thin and tooled, gleamed against the gold of her skin.

"Lovely." His voice was guttural, deep, and rumbled against her skin as he leaned forward and nuzzled her belly, licking her navel as he reached around her and cupped her ass.

"Irian…" Tyriel gasped out his name as he caught her in his arms before she could slide to the floor, and he spread the lips of her sex and licked her.

"Tasty little elf," he said wickedly, carrying her to the bed. He spread her out, pushing her thighs wide, running his hands over the gleaming black leather before opening her with his thumbs and staring down at her, at the wet, pink folds, naked of hair except for a small neat little patch just at her pubic bone. "Pretty little elf." He lowered his head and caught her clit in his mouth, catching her hands and pinning them down as she tried to squirm away and close her thighs.

Working two thick fingers inside her slippery, tight channel, he worked her ruthlessly to climax, suckling on her clit, fucking her tight, hungry body, and shuddering when she climaxed into his hand with a sob. Lifting up, he studied her, his face wet and gleaming from her cream. "You didna say my name."

She was still shuddering and whimpering from climax as he quickly jerked his clothes off, revealing a long, pale body rippling with muscles and marked with scars from battle. His cock sprang free from his tight, laced up trousers, thick, ruddy, rising from a thatch of golden hair, a gleaming drop seeping from it as he advanced on her. Her eyes blurred and for a moment, she saw another man, broader, dark gold skin, long waist length hair, black as her own, tumbled with curls, a more battle-scarred body, gypsy-dark eyes.

Tyriel was still gasping for air, hardly able to breathe as he grasped her hands, jerked them over her head, pinning her down. He wedged a muscled thigh between her legs, spreading her thighs open and nudging at her cleft with his cock. "Who is touching you, lass?" he murmured as he lowered his head to take a reddened nipple into his mouth.

Straining against his grasp, a sob fell past her lips. He pushed her nipple against the roof of his mouth and suckled deep, rolling his eyes upward to stare at her. Hot and wicked, his tongue and teeth worked the nipple into one aching point of pleasure until she was whimpering and squirming from just the lightest touch of his tongue on her flesh.

She stared down into his eyes, and the other image superimposed on Aryn, and stayed this time—dark, dark eyes, inky black curls spilling across her body, his free hand cupping her ass.

A hair-thin scar bisected his left eyebrow, and another sliced down his right shoulder…scars she had never noticed before. He rasped, demanded, "Who touches you?" as he kissed a blazing line of kisses between her breasts and locked his teeth around the other nipple drawing it tight and listening to her gasp.

"Irian…"

With a ragged groan, he tore his mouth from her breast and positioned himself at the wet, swollen entrance to her pussy, staring down into her eyes. "Years, I have waited. Years without end." Then he said nothing else as he slowly forged his way into her body, his thick, hard length slicing through her as she stared helplessly, fascinated, into his eyes, arms stretched overhead, ragged gasps falling from her lips.

She was begging by the time he was buried inside her, pleading and rocking against him, whipping her head back and forth. His cock jerked within her sheath and she whimpered, the muscles in her pussy tightening around him hungrily as she rocked against him. Slowing, Irian lowered his body down atop her, and why did it seem so much heavier? Aryn's body was still there, wasn't it? Everything felt so different, his weight, the feel of his body, the texture of his hair, even his taste. Her mind spun out of control and she sobbed as his mouth covered hers, feeling his cock jerk within her sheath. His hand released her wrists, trailed down the length of her arms, over the side of her breast, her ribcage and waist as he shifted his weight. She felt the phantom brush of his fingers on her clit and she screamed into his mouth as he started to ride her, filling her with hard, deep thrusts of his cock, a groan vibrating from his chest.

He shifted his angle, moving higher on her body so that each thrust hit that bed of nerves buried by the mouth of her womb. Tyriel's pussy convulsed around him rhythmically and Irian growled against her mouth, rising up to his knees, grabbing her legs, spreading them wide, holding her open with one hand behind each knee as he stared down at her, watching as he pushed his thick, dark cock between the plump wet lips of her sex, his lids low and hooded over his dark eyes.

With short deep digs of his hips, he filled her, staring down into her eyes hungrily, greedily. "Ye canna know how long I've waited for ye," he muttered. Her eyes locked with his, captivated, as he released one of her legs and trailed his hand down her body. "Days, months, years without end." Thumb and forefinger closed around one dark rose-red nipple and he plucked it, smiling as she arched with a weak scream. "Such a pretty, pretty thing…wild, wild gypsy-elf. So tight, so wet, soft as silk, sweet…"

Tyriel's head was spinning. Her heart pounded in her chest, heavy and hard, echoing the slow, pounding thrusts of his cock inside her vagina as he pushed into her. The tight wet clasp of her sex hugged his cock, clung to him as he pulled out and surged back inside. His hand slid further down her body and pinched her clit, then rotated over it in sure steady strokes until her pussy started to convulse around him.

He growled, bending low and wrapping his arms tightly around her, bracing her weight for his thrusts with a steely, corded embrace and banding her against his heavy length as he started to shudder. Against her hair, he started to groan. "My name...who am I?"

But Tyriel barely heard him as she fisted her hands in the silky skeins of his raven-black hair, the climax inside her womb exploding outward and arching her up until she was screaming and bucking against him, cream sliding from her, coating his cock, the muscles in her pussy locking down rhythmically around his sex and stroking him into climax as she screamed out his name.

Moments later, she sighed as he stroked her hair and soothed her into sleep. His name slid from her lips one final time as she slid into slumber. "Irian..."

The guilt in his gut faded away to a dull ache as he wrapped his arms around her and rested.

He didn't really sleep, not even in this body. He hovered in a semiconscious state that charged his mind and magick, and allowed his soul to wander, his mind to remember. So much to remember, and so very little that was pleasant. When Irian dragged himself back to the present, he was aware of Tyriel's firm little ass, snug against his cock, the sweet scent of her hair, those wild Jiupsu curls spilling all over his arms and chest, tickling his chin. His cock throbbed against her ass, a sweet ache, one he hadn't had the luxury of feeling in years.

Ahhh…what was he to do? He could not allow the lass to leave. Such danger lurked for her. The blackness crowded at the very edges of Irian's mind, his soul. Such a powerful thing she was…how could he force her into staying? If she wasn't elvin, he could make her, physically, though such a thing sickened him. But the elf-kind were strong, stronger than mortal men.

She must stay safe…they needed her.

She murmured and sighed in her sleep.

The swordsman's name.

A slow smile crept across Irian's face.

She fled for fear the swordsman did not love her.

Aryn loved her well and truly, and even he knew it. It was his own mortality he feared.

If the daft fool would simply open his blind eyes…he lowered his mouth to Tyriel's naked shoulder, the black curls tangling with and mingling with hers until he couldn't tell where her hair ended and his began. Gripping one naked hip in his big, scarred hand, he pressed a hot, opened-mouthed kiss to her shoulder and started to pump his cock against the curve of her ass, using the heat and touch of his body to distract her as magick started to whisper through the air.

Blond hair spilled across Tyriel's body, straight, thick, golden as the sun. Firm strong hands rolled her over and deep, deep blue eyes caught hers as those hands captured her face and his mouth found hers, his tongue pushing deep inside her mouth, bringing that unique taste. His body, lean, powerful, pale, covered hers and his thigh wedged between hers as he murmured her name against her mouth, that soft raspy voice, thick with sleep, sending chills down her spine. His hands raced over her body, cupped her breasts, pinched her nipples, plucked them. His hot, wet mouth closed over them and Tyriel sobbed out his name, reaching up, fisting her hands in his thick golden hair.

His teeth bit down on one nipple and she screamed, arching up. One hand cupped her, and one thick finger worked its way into the tight, slippery channel of her sex and she shuddered. His groan reverberated against her breast, sending another shudder through her body.

The fog clouding her brain was slowly, reluctantly lifting and she pushed at his shoulders. "Aryn?"

"Shh..."

His mouth covered hers again and he moved back up her body and gripped her thighs with his hands, pushing deep inside her body with one driving thrust. She moaned, the tight, wet clasp of her pussy closing over him in welcome as he surged forward, deeper and deeper until he was buried inside her to the hilt, the head of his cock resting against the mouth of her womb. She felt his fingers threading through her hair, his hands cupping the back of her head, magick whispering through the room, wild, and untamed.

"Aryn...ahh...all I've ever yearned..." She sobbed against his mouth as he ate at hers hungrily, his tongue sweeping and tangling with hers, withdrawing so that he could nibble at her lower lip. Pushing his tongue back inside, past her lips and teeth, he greedily took in as much of her taste as he could.

Wild magick…

Tyriel screamed against his mouth as he moved higher on her body, rubbing against the sensitized bud of her clit with each thrust of his hips. She reached down, dug her nails into the taut curve of his ass and pulled him more tightly against her, rocking her hips up, taking him as deeply as she could. She felt the rasp of his cock inside her, raking her swollen, wet tissues, the rounded blunt head passing over the sweetly hidden area inside, and she whimpered against his mouth, her head falling limply back.

Through the veil of her lashes, she stared up at him as he pushed up onto his hands, planting them beside her head, staring down at her with dark, hooded eyes of midnight-blue, that golden hair falling like silk around his strong, broad shoulders, raining down his back. Her eyes trailed down his body, lingered over his chest, the sculpted form of his pectorals, gleaming with a fine sheen of sweat before moving down to the bunching and flexing of his belly as he pumped his cock inside her.

Her breath caught inside her throat, staring down at it as he drove that long ruddy column of flesh back inside the wet well of her sex. A hungry, helpless whimper fell from her lips and she reached up, clutching at his shoulders, her eyes staring raptly at their joined bodies, his cock gleaming with her cream, slowly drawing out and pushing back inside.

On the third slow thrust in, she climaxed with a scream, the muscles in her vagina clamping down around his cock rhythmically, her hips jerking, her heart racing. Magick broke open inside and flooded the room.

His cock jerked within the tight grasp of her pussy and she felt the hot jet of his seed fill her as she started to drift back down.

It wasn't until she was sliding back into sleep that something started to niggle at her mind.

Something wasn't right.

There had been free magick before she climaxed.

Tyriel may lose control when she climaxed, but rarely. Now if she willingly dropped her control, that was another thing altogether.

And while the enchanter's magick was slowly filling Aryn, it had not yet taken hold of him completely.

The magick had not been Aryn's.

Irian…

You bloody bastard.

She knew he was trying to protect her.

If the darkness looming at her mind didn't frighten her so, she might have been angry. But even with that blackness, Tyriel could not stay. Slowly, she sat up, wincing as muscles rarely used so vigorously went on vicious protest. Behind her, Aryn slept on, deeply. Irian forcing himself into Aryn's body had drained both of them and that, at least, would work in Tyriel's favor.

She reached up and stroked the amber moonstone between her breasts. Her nipples grew tight in the cool morning air as she rose gingerly, still stroking the pendant.

It was time to go home.

She'd visit the cousins in Bentyl first, pay her respects there.

But then…home.

To Averne, where she belonged.

Dawn wasn't even a thought when she slipped out of the room, looking over her shoulder at Aryn's nude body sprawled across the sheets. He was inhumanly beautiful, more than even the elvin kin. The muscled curve of his ass, the long muscled lines of his back, his long golden hair hanging in a glorious tangle down his back and across his shoulder, one strand lying across the sharp edge of his cheek.

Damn you, Irian…what a memory to leave me with.

A hot, bitter wash of pain filled her chest and throat and she turned away, closing the door in silence. The heels of her hard-soled elvish boots were soundless on the wooden floors as she moved down the hall and the stairs.

Tears burned her eyes and a lingering ache throbbed between her thighs, inside her cleft. Riding wasn't going to be such a pleasant act today. "Kilidare, you had best behave yourself," she said aloud as she headed down the already busy streets. In her mind's eyes, she could feel the mount's interest, almost see his ears perk up.

And she never noticed the shadow moving up behind her.

Kilidare was worried.

His breed wasn't horse.

And his breed was far more intelligent than a mere horse. He could run like the wind, track like a hound, puzzle and reason like a primate, but he needed a focus.

He needed his mistress.

And when his mistress didn't appear right away, he forgot his worry after a time and he started to wander away.

The elvin steeds were originally wild.

What separated the elvin steeds from their wild forebears were their masters.

So he started to roam. But he waited and he remembered her.

Time passed, though. Their bond stretched ever thinner as he roamed the woods and plains of the area around the towne of Ifteril. She could still come. She would. She always did.

Chapter Nine

Her eyes were swollen, battered. Nearly impossible to open from the beating she had taken only hours before. An elf's healing abilities made a human's look laughable. Within three days, the marks from the beating would be all but gone. But it was draining.

The iron at her wrists, at her ankles, wrapped around her belly was sickening her. And the collar around her neck, a slave's collar.

On a Princess.

The blood of a Royal, which she so rarely acknowledged, was so very, very enraged — the death of this man must be painful enough, slow enough, bloody enough.

He had put a slave's collar on an elvish Princess, the daughter of gypsy chieftains.

She stared blankly at the man in front of her.

Tainan.

Her mouth twisted in a snarl when he came through the door.

"Are you ready to yield?" he purred.

"Haik ilo biloi nu takimi," she spat. *I'd rather fuck a goat.* Since she hissed the words into his mind as well as through her busted teeth, her meaning was quite clear.

"Will you yield?" He turned and lifted a whip, topped with little metal balls. "I've broken better mages than you. You were foolish, wandering around unshielded, alone. I could smell the stink of that man on you. Perhaps I should have waited before taking you, shouldn't have beaten you so cruelly. Ahh, but that's in the past. Will you yield?"

"Will you die a thousand and three painfully slow deaths?" she rasped, her throat achingly dry.

The whip lifted and flew, and her shrieks filled the room.

Tainan purred, "And now you are trapped."

"*Va takimi*," she muttered. She turned her head aside and withdrew into herself. She barely managed to close the door inside her mind by the time the second blow fell.

She took the first month of abuse with almost good humor. She wasn't De Asir, but she had trained with them. And the legendary assassins knew how to take abuse and torture, for years and months on end.

But Tainan was after something.

And once she realized what it was, she broke inside.

It wasn't her body, or even her blood.

She could have taken the abuse, the rapes, and the starvation.

But it wasn't just that he was after, though he reveled in her suffering, drinking it and feeding from it, the way a demon could feed from blood.

It was her magick, her knowledge, her soul.

He was a soul eater.

Tyriel fell back away from the black shadows that came to her, reaching for her, touching her, grabbing her. A scream fell from her lips, terrified and broken, and she slashed out with magick even though she had sworn not to. The iron on her body burned her with every bit of magick she used, and it blinded her, deafened her, sickened her, weakened her.

He would get her.

Eventually. Her fear would break her.

She fled inside herself and wrapped herself in the lights of the magick that made her what she was, the sorcery, the mage gift, letting the bright, burning lights warm her. She felt safe here—which was laughable. As long as these lights burned, he would torture her, pursue her, try to take her soul.

As long as they burned.

If the lights went out—

It was forbidden.

"Da..." she called out to him, but the stone around her neck that bound her to him had been taken and smashed. And some power blocked her from him. She was alone. Well, and truly, for the first time in her life, completely alone.

She knew what she must do. But was so terribly afraid of it.

Some of the kin could not even manage what she was thinking. It was dangerous. It was deadly. It was beyond foolish.

But if the magick was not there...

She could not let him take her soul. She could not. He would have too much, too many secrets, knowledge of the elvin kin, the haunts and hiding places of the clans. No, he could not have those. And Irian. Ahh, the damage he could do with a blade like that.

To have Irian, Aryn must die.

No.

It was with a shuddering, frightened spirit that she reached out to the first light, and put it out.

Chapter Ten

Aryn stood outside the gates of Ifteril and closed his eyes. The last place to look. There was little else left to do after this.

"As though ye intend t' stop lookin'," Irian murmured. The enchanter stood at his side, his long hair in a thick braid that hung over his shoulder. He seemed so solid at times, it often surprised Aryn that no other seemed to notice him. *"We will find her. Something here will be leadin' us t' the elf, I know."*

Aryn's hands closed into tight fists. "I never should have let her leave. You knew this would happen. Why didn't I listen?"

"We didna know she would drop off the face o' the earth, or that she would slip away in the dead of the night. I tried, truly, to convince her t' stay."

"I bet," Aryn muttered sourly, sliding the long-dead warrior a bitter glance. The question was how?

The gypsy at Aryn's side barely blinked when the mercenary started talking seemingly to himself. Kellen had learned that the swordsman had odd ways, to put it mildly. He would wake at night and ride in silence to a towne miles and miles away, find a young child cowering in fear from a man about ready to rape and beat—Kellen shoved that from his mind.

That particular child was safe with the clans now.

As were a number of others who had appeared with Tyriel over the years, since she had taken up with the swordsman. It was the blade. That enchanted blade. Kellen's da had been a mage and while Kellen was not gifted, he knew how the craft worked, had the sight of it, if not the powers. And his eyes itched every bloody time he looked at the sword.

And when he looked toward Aryn, sometimes he thought he was damn well going insane. He would catch a sight, just behind his eyelids, like nothing he had ever seen, a long towering powerful gypsy with yards of wildly curling hair and a savage smile, and eyes so achingly sad it made Kellen's heart hurt.

And then it was gone.

Kellen glanced at Aryn now and asked, "To the inn?"

Passing a hand over his eyes, Aryn nodded. "The inn is really all we have to work with. Tyriel was here but a few days. Irian had ways of keeping up with her. He knew when she had left us."

Kellen knew when the man's attention had left him again. Talking to the Soul inside the sword again. With a sigh, Kellen brushed aside the itchy feeling it gave him and followed the tall swordsman to the towne gates, boldly meeting the guard's eyes with a smirk as the guard studied the gypsy appraisingly.

"Like a hole in our souls, she left. Do ye admit it yet, swordsman? That she is yours?"

"I always cared, always wanted her." Aryn tossed the enchanter a snarl. "But why pledge my heart and soul to a woman who will still be young when I am no more than dust in the ground? Why wish that grief upon her? Do you think I did not realize she cared? And could do more?"

"Your foolishness has cost you and her much. And my silence hasna helped." Irian retreated back into himself, gone in less than a blink, a cold wind of grief blowing across Aryn's body as they came to the inn where they had last seen Tyriel all of twelve months past. A night he didn't remember, when Irian had swarmed up and taken over — what had happened?

Ah...his body remembered. His cock thickened and swelled, pressing against the lacings of his leather breeches, blood pulsing thick in his veins, the whisper of her scent flooding his nostrils.

An image assaulted him.

Her beaten starving body, mauled and scarred, her eyes so dim and lackluster.

No power on earth — his hands closed into fists and the blade at his back felt heavy.

No power on earth would stop him from finding the one who had done this.

Blood-red hair, blood-red mouth, pale, pale skin, blood magick.

Tainan...

"Aryn?"

"Wait," Aryn whispered, his voice low and harsh. His lids lowered until only bare slits of his eyes showed and his breath came in harsh gasps as he remembered that night six years earlier. Jaren, Tyriel and he, in the bowels of the city as they sought the man who wanted to sacrifice another innocent to the Darkness Below.

Tainan.

His prey had a face.

Aryn woke in the silence of the night with a blade pressed to his throat.

"I trusted you, mortal. Into your hands, I gave my princess, to love, and keep and protect. And my Lord Prince tells me she is gone, away from his power, his touch. For six long months I have searched for her." The low, almost silent whisper brought a dread fear into Aryn's belly but he threw it off and opened his eyes, staring into Jaren's dark face.

The elf moved away and threw a mage light into the air, staring at Aryn with glittering, angry eyes. "Six long months. Six months is nothing to the kin. Nothing unless you seek what is dear to your heart, as Tyriel is to me. I trusted her to you. And you did not keep her safe. For that I should kill you where you lay."

Aryn sat up slowly, staring at the elf as Irian came out of the darkness, wavering into view, solidifying and staring at the elf with cool eyes.

"And three months, I have searched for you, swordsman. And then I was led here and I have waited. Waited here. Now you arrive," Jaren murmured as he drew his blade and ran one finger down the deadly edge, ignoring the enchanter.

Aryn felt the cold fear sliding through his belly as the assassin continued to stare at him with gleaming green eyes that glowed and shifted with a morass of colors and magick that swelled from within. There was a power there, like what he had sensed inside the half-elf, but it was more deadly, finer, focused—all of it focused on him. "I know who has her. Are you here to fight this out with me, or here to help me save her, you long-eared son-of-a-bitch?" he asked in a low, harsh voice.

A flash of teeth lit the elf's poetically beautiful face and Jaren threw back his head, his long, razor-straight hair falling down his back as his musical laughter filled the air. "'Tis no wonder the Princess was so drawn. Not a bit o' fear in you. And so very unmortal do you act." Then he moved like a streak of lightning across the room.

Aryn fell back on the bed, rolled backward and landed on the balls of his feet, barely managing to draw his blade and lift it before Jaren was at his back. In such close quarters, a sword did little good. Unless it was enchanted. A long knife at his throat, Aryn breathed shallowly as Jaren whispered silkily, "Where is my lady Princess?"

"Go fuck yourself and the bloody steed that brought you here, you magicked son-of-a-whore." Aryn didn't bother to reach for the hands that held him. Jaren was centuries old. He slashed his roughened palm down the blade as Irian stood watching it all with what looked like very amused eyes. *"So nice of you to help me here."*

"Oh, it's not your death he wants. He's just bloody pissed. If he tries t' kill ye, I'll stop him." Irian leaned back against the wall and crossed his arms over his broad chest, lifting a curious brow as Jaren continued to ignore what Aryn did with the blade. Was the elf truly so ignorant of what Aryn did?

Aryn mouthed the words silently and too late, Jaren felt the magick rustle through the air just before the air above Aryn's body grew fire hot. Aryn whirled away just as Jaren fell back silently, the front of his body scorched and smoking. Most men would have been screaming in pain, but the elf just stared appraisingly at the swordsman before lifting his reddened hands and studying the blackened, blistered flesh that was forming. "What an interesting change," he mused.

"Tyriel is not your lady."

Jaren purred, "And pray tell, why not?"

Irian perked up with interest as Aryn lifted the blade and pointed it at the elf and said harshly, "She is mine."

The firelight flickered across Aryn's face, casting half of it in shadow as he sat staring into the night. Irian had swarmed up from the recesses of his mind and forced his damnable will upon Aryn's body until Aryn sullenly agreed to stop for the night. They had ridden for three days straight and the blasted elf looked as rested, and as out for blood, when they stopped as when they started.

He lay on his bedroll, smoking a long, oddly scented pipe, stroking a crescent-shaped metallic stone of black at his neck as Aryn stared into the night.

The swordsman had no idea how closely the elf was watching him. And likely wouldn't care either.

He had sat for the longest time alone, undisturbed, aware of nothing but a sense of her...somewhere in the east. Closer and closer.

Now Irian was at his side, lowering himself to his haunches, his rough-hewn features puzzled, curious, almost too afraid to hope. His voice, when rarely he spoke in a voice for somebody other than Aryn alone to hear, had a deep, rippling quality, like a stone cast into a well. "I sense something...Tyriel...but not her. I know not what." Irian glanced over as the elf rose to his feet in one smooth graceful movement, his muscled body gleaming in the firelight. "It sensed me. Doesna know me. Mayhap you, swordsman. Come."

Aryn was already mounting Bel bareback.

Irian disappeared into the night, inside Aryn, guiding him to the source of what he had sensed.

When Aryn slid from his mount sometime later, what he saw pacing in the moonlight was the last thing he had ever expected.

The elvish stallion was taller, broader than Bel, with larger eyes that had the uncanny, unsettling ability of glowing. It resembled a horse, the way a tame housecat resembled a wild mountain lion that a faerie minx had tamed. But this elvish steed looked very unlike the mount Aryn had seen just months earlier. His neatly groomed coat had grown long and shabby, his eyes no longer had that 'settled' look in them. He looked vaguely wild and lost as he turned considering eyes Aryn's way.

He looked...wild.

But he kept cocking his head at Aryn as the swordsman slid one leg over Bel's head and circled the clearing, his intelligent eyes trained on the swordsman's face, rapt and fascinated. Curious. Hungry.

And then Jaren charged in, lips peeled back from his teeth in a snarl as he launched himself in a low tumble at the elvish stallion that ended with him underneath the beast, a long wicked blade drawn and ready.

His own mount went nearly wild, pawing at the air, his screams filling the night.

Aryn kicked Jaren's wrist, hard enough, he hoped, to numb it and grabbed the elf's ankle, hauling him out from under the stallion.

"He betrayed his mistress," Jaren snarled, flipping to his feet, snarling at Aryn and whirling back to the stallion.

"He looks rather lost to me." Aryn turned back to the stallion, rubbing the beast's black face, his cheeks and neck with gentle hands, staring into the dazed, helpless eyes. *"Pretty mistress...good hands...she never came..."*

The voice filled the air.

Astoundingly clear in their minds. Even Jaren stumbled back in shock from it.

Aryn said softly, "Tyriel. She was coming to you that morning. She never came, did she?"

"The elvish mounts are fantastic creatures, but none can comprehend that well." Jaren moved again in Kilidare's direction. "'Tis like a guard dog. And he sorely failed at his job."

"Nevernevernevernever."

Aryn ran his hand again down Kilidare's cheek and slid Jaren a look. "We go to find her. The lady. The pretty lady with the good hands, your mistress."

"Evil man, evil dark take...I scent...not see...but his scent I know."

"Evil man?" Jaren asked, stopping in his tracks. "How do you know his scent?"

"Towne, demon mark...all over her. His scent, all over. He take, I feel, then pretty mistress gone."

Jaren's face was blank, simply stunned.

Aryn smothered a smile as he continued to stroke Kilidare, soothing the bewildered stallion. "We will find her," Aryn murmured soothingly as the great beast rested his head over Aryn's shoulder, a huge shudder wracking him.

* * * * *

Tyriel knew the end was finally slipping nearer.

Her heart was failing her.

She lay wearily on the cold floor, feeling it stutter and slow. It didn't hurt. She had feared heart failure would be painful, like it was for humans. But the elvish in her had won out again. It was merely...slipping away. Ever slowing beats and eventually she would drift into a sleep that could linger for days or weeks.

Without the treatments her people knew, she would be dead within a month. And mostly likely even those would not help. Human or elvish will made up for so much.

And she had no will left. No desire left to live and suffer and fight.

There was a brush on the edges of her mind that felt oddly familiar as she drifted closer to sleep.

But she was too tired to think about it.

And the crashing of doors, the burning smoke didn't faze her at all.

The low, sprawling, lavishly built house wasn't at all what Aryn expected. When the songs were sung of heroes heroically rescuing the Princess, it was from a towering, craggy cliff, or a cave buried deep in a jungle.

But the steed had started to liven, and purpose had returned to his eyes. This was where he had led them, where Aryn's heart and soul had been guiding him. They had stumbled through a thick, obscuring fog that tasted metallic, almost poisonous, burning and stinging Aryn's eyes. "'Tis illusion," Jaren said quietly from atop his mount. His dark-green eyes shifted to a paler color as power rolled through them. One hand lifted and his fingers spread, flexed, and a mist of light formed, then dissipated.

"A protection. It hides something."

The something had been this place, this house. After the light had dissipated from Jaren's hand, the fog surrounding them had started to lift. And as they moved, it lifted ever more until they moved into a circle of free air. By midday, it was all gone. And at nightfall, they came to the edge of a clearing in the woods and that low sprawling structure came into view. In the light of the full moon, Jaren said, "I feel her, her strength wanes."

And the stallion near went mad, scenting her. Aryn could feel her, too.

The strategist in him would prefer a plan of sorts.

Jaren slid him a narrow look, his eyes gleaming like a cat's in the dark. "As would I, swordsman. But her time runs short. I did not leave my Princess with good words between us. She is young, too young, too good a woman to die in such a place as this. And I know this scent—'tis my fault she is in there. If I had kept my bond. At the time, I did not believe he would come seeking her so quickly."

Aryn lifted a brow, quizzically.

And Jaren laughed. "You are in the presence of one of the few psychic warriors known among the kin, swordsman. How else do you think I knew you were in the city?"

Irian was oddly quiet.

The blade at Aryn's back was becoming heavier, the way it had in the early years, before Aryn had realized just what he held when he first took up the blade. *"Know you, friend, it grieves me that it led to this. If I had known she would come to any danger, any pain…never would I have risked her, never."* As they crept closer, their presence muffled by the deft touch of elvin magick, Irian spoke somberly into Aryn's mind.

"It's not your fault, Irian. Tyriel has always done what Tyriel wants to do—and her actions shouldn't have put her at risk, but they did. That isn't your fault."

"Ahhh, but my wanting her so desperately clouded my thinking…"

Aryn slid the enchanter a wry glance as Irian walked through a tree without blinking an eye. "You love her," Aryn said quietly. "Don't think I don't know it. Don't act like I'm not aware. The person who is to blame is Tainan. And Tainan alone. Not you. Not me, though I will kick my ass from now until the day I die. And certainly not Tyriel."

"Do not be so quick to acquit me, brother of my soul. There are things you canna know about me. Things I havna told a living soul in more millenia than even I can recall."

Aryn drew the blade at the door. Jaren took the back. Very few servants were here. Very few living souls. But many, many magicked traps and creatures. As Aryn drew the blade, he also called Irian, pulling the enchanter willingly inside himself, so that the two were one inside his skin. Five mortals. Including the most important one. Tainan Delre.

And the ever-weakening soul of a very battered elf.

Aryn launched himself at the door, words he didn't know he knew pouring from him. And not a drop of blood was spilled, not a grain of salt flung on the ground. The magick was well and firmly inside him, and in his rage the accoutrements so many enchanters needed were forgotten. Irian smiled bitterly. His task was nearly complete. But at such a high cost.

Fire erupted the moment Aryn's body touched the door. At the same time, the very foundation of the building shook as Jaren's magick breached the barriers that surrounded and protected it. Under the onslaught, it buckled.

A berzerker, Aryn lifted his sword and cut through one guard, severing his torso from the waist up, leaving him still screaming from the shock of it as he realized he was dead. His eyes gleamed red with rage as he scented Tyriel on the body of the huge man who came running at him, blade drawn. Aryn flung one hand up, slicing it along Asrel's edge for blood, smearing his blood on the face of the man who stopped, frozen in abject terror at the sight of the warrior standing before him with death and vengeance in his glowing blue eyes. The images continued to shift— from a tall slender blond man, who looked almost angelic, like an avenging angel, to a sinister-looking, towering warrior of a man with wildly curling black hair and rough-hewn features in barbaric garb, a wicked smile on his face, the very devil to prey upon your fears.

The guard screamed and screamed, as the man rubbed a smear of blood down his cheek, then impaled him on the tip of the sword, pushing it in slowly from his belly, downward. "Why is it I smell her on you? All over you?" Aryn asked hoarsely, his rage tightening his throat. As the blade forged through his internal organs, it burned them, searing them, charring them. "My lady—you beat her, raped her and whipped her. If I could spare the time..." A growl ripped from his throat as he twisted the blade.

The blade scraped over the guard's internal sex organs, and then outward, and his screams locked in his throat. "Die...slowly," and he jerked the blade forward, ripping bone, tissue, muscle, and the man's cock from his body.

In the hall, Aryn came face to face with Tainan.

Jaren had planned on taking this bastard.

But both Irian and Aryn had other plans. Of course, Tyriel was more important, but if they happened upon him…

"Bury Asrel deep inside his black heart, my brother. Such a simple blow, and he will not expect a physical attack from an enchanter."

Irian formed. Larger than life, full of vengeance, rage, anger, his black hair whipping around his face, and he flung a painful lash into Tainan's face, distracting him as Aryn lunged. "I don't need distraction tactics to kill him."

"She hasna the time…do it."

And so he did, lunging full-on, but pausing to deliver an arm-numbing blow to Tainan's face, taking him to the ground and straddling him as the man went flying back. Aryn pierced his chest, driving Asrel through his heart, twisting it around, turning that black, worthless, shriveled, evil thing into so much meat until thick blood bubbled up through Tainan's mouth.

"Now, we must hurry. The magicks may fall without him here to hold."

Chapter Eleven

Jaren lifted her broken body in his arms, feeling his throat tighten. *Ah, sweet. I failed you, didn't I?*

If he had kept his promise, his bond sooner, but he had thought he had time. Five years, he had spent five years watching the young Larel heal, then blossom, and enchant him.

And it had cost Tyriel.

She might yet die with bitterness between them.

Their last words had been in anger, and she had battled down a demon while Jaren stood with a child in his arms, watching, too angry with her to offer assistance. It didn't matter that she didn't need it. It mattered that he had not offered. Even now, she bore the demon's silver mark on her breast, her frail skinny body sallow, the silver mark nearly gray now. Her black hair, always so glossy and soft, was brittle and dry, lifeless.

Her heart was failing her.

Because he had blamed her for not letting him rush to Larel's side. And if he had...Larel would have been killed outright. He had wanted to be Larel's savior. Instead it had been all of them. His pride—was that to blame? As he carried Tyriel out into the clean-smelling night air, he rested his chin on her hair and clenched his jaw against the grief that rose up in his chest.

If he had gone after Tainan instead of mooning after a bewitching mortal-fae—Larel—Tyriel would not be lying so near death's door. The metal at her waist, her wrists, her ankles weakened her. It would have killed Jaren, or another full-blood. If they could get those off, get her onto clean earth to buy them time...he felt a big warm nose nuzzling his arm. *"My lady...help her..."*

The house behind him was starting to fall into the earth. Aryn had destroyed Tainan. And much magick had been woven into that house. The entire building would fall now that the master of it was dead. Lifting his gleaming green eyes to the elvish stallion he said softly, "Help her I will try. But I am no healer, Kilidare."

The stallion pawed the ground and tossed his great head.

"Kilidare help her. Kilidare heal."

He donned a pair of thin leather gloves and pulled a pair of lock picks from his belt before he went to work on the iron. Within moments, he was tossing the damnable stuff to the side, away from Tyriel and himself as the steed curled his body around his broken, battered mistress.

"She is badly hurt, not just her body." Staring into the dark eyes of the steed, Jaren pulled a vial of vesna oil out and went to work on the angry red and blackened flesh that had formed under the metal bands.

Not her body I fear for, but her mind.

That was how Aryn found them, Tyriel's battered body cupped in the curve of her protective stallion's body, his head arched impossibly around to nuzzle her belly and arm and face as magick and power crawled through the air. He knew the feel and scent of it by now, but didn't quite trust his mind. "Irian, am I going mad or is the horse working magick?"

Irian chuckled as he shimmered into view. "*Stranger things have happened. Kilidare is no more a mere horse than ye are a mere human. Ye stopped being merely human within three o' four years o' wieldin' an enchanted blade. Kilidare is an elvish steed, and may resemble a horse on the outside, but all similarity ends there. Heard tales, I have, of warrior-trained elvish steeds, who had no masters, who were their own masters.*"

Aryn moved his eyes back to Kilidare and slowly shook his head. *Healing horses? What is bloody next?*

He knelt at her side, cupping her face in his hands, feeling a rage unlike anything he had ever known tear through him, side by side with grief, and relief.

She was alive.

She was battered and bruised and beaten and scarred.

She was alive.

Her lids lifted slowly and he saw the dullness there, the lack of realization before her lids drifted down again.

She was broken.

It made sense, really, when Jaren thought it through later. The blasted brat of a Princess had an elvish stallion that had never really needed taming, that had sought her out, instead of her seeking him out. She had taken mortal wounds that would have killed even their kind and was up and riding around with a sassy smile on her lovely face within two days.

And the odd almost insane look he had seen in the stallion's eyes, once he had calmed enough to think back on it—they had bonded. Not just as mistress and beast. But as magick-makers in the soul. Tyriel had been the stallion's focus, had made him more than a wild beast, like all the elvish steeds. Just this particular steed had magick in his blood, and it made him more unpredictable than most, more untamed.

Jaren stared impassively into Aryn's eyes.

"I thought you said the bloody horse was going to heal her!"

Jaren narrowed his eyes as the swordsman stepped just a little closer and snarled into his face just a little louder. "You push your luck, mortal," he said warningly.

"We are wasting our time. She needs healing–and we've already sat here all of yesterday and all of last night. Will we wait another day and night as well?" Aryn demanded, reaching out and grabbing Jaren's tunic. The soft, molded leather bunched under his hands and Aryn yanked him forward. "Remember your word to her. You swore to kill her if her hesitation cost a child's life? If yours has cost Tyriel her life, I'll be holding you accountable."

Aryn bared his teeth in a grim smile before he stepped back, sliding out of reach just as Jaren moved to strike. Aryn laughed easily. "No longer quite so human, Irian is telling me. I'll never be wholly anything, but no longer human. And I was never your mere mortal."

The assassin's blade was wickedly long and sharp. Deadly, and Aryn knew it could pierce his flesh as easily as a fork could slide through butter, but he'd made his point. He threw up a deflector's ward just in case Jaren decided to throw it, but he suspected the man was brandishing it just to make a point—if the elf wanted it, he would be dead before he saw it coming.

Jaren acknowledged it with a raised brow and waited for Aryn.

Now that both points were driven home, so to speak, they could get on with the business of what really mattered. Tyriel.

"My loyalty, my love for her has never been in doubt." The elvish lord's hands moved and the blade was gone as quickly as it had appeared, as though it had never existed. "Though our last parting was not a pleasant one, my Princess knows me well. Doubtless, she knows how foolish I feel. I would move the stars from the sky to save her, and well she knows this."

Aryn snarled. "And you show it by letting her lie in a forest with a horse?"

Irian chose at that moment to whisper reprovingly to Aryn alone, *"The True One chooses odd bearers for His powers. Is it our place to judge those bearers?"*

Jaren coolly said, "He has healed her ills before. I will take all chances, any chance to save her. However—"

A heartrending shriek tore through the air. Followed by the sound of weeping, gut-wrenching sobs that filled the air. Jaren murmured quietly as Aryn took off running, "The stallion succeeded in healing her body. It is up to you, now, to heal her heart and soul."

Aryn burst into the clearing, his heart hammering in his chest, lungs burning to find Tyriel sobbing, alone in the center of the clearing, arms wrapped pitifully around herself, rocking back and forth. Kilidare stood to the side, shifting on his feet, head low, keening sadly in his throat. Her back—narrow, dirty, scarred—shook with the force of her sobs and Aryn's nails bit into his skin.

He hadn't made him pay enough.

Can we fetch his dark soul from hell and do it again?

Oddly enough, as he moved in his woman's direction, he realized, he was alone. Completely. Irian was not there at all.

"Tyriel."

That soft, deep voice rolled over her skin like a caress, but it wasn't real.

Simply couldn't be.

"Tyriel, sweet, open your eyes and look at me," he whispered roughly as a callused, warm hand gently stroked the side of her arm before moving away.

She scuttled away from the touch.

"Love, he's gone. Dead. He cannot touch you ever again, I swear."

Gone? Dead?

She shook her head. It was too much. That voice was lying, sounding too much like the one she longed for, telling her things she had hoped and prayed for. It had to be a dream—

"Sweet, open your eyes." The voice was firmer now and two large, warm hands worked their way into her hair, forcing her to lift her head, gently, very gently, but so very firmly. She had no choice but to lift her head and look into impossibly blue eyes, surrounded by thick black lashes, tipped with gold, eyes that were diamond-bright, wet, haunted, tormented and angry and grieving.

"No." she whispered hoarsely. "You're not real."

A smile curved his mouth upward as he lowered his lips to hers, and his entire body seemed to shudder, in relief? In joy? "Oh, but I am, my lady," he murmured against her lips. "Quite real."

"Illusion."

"Then denounce me," he offered, stroking his hands down her arms, running the tips of his fingers over her lips, the arch of her brows, as though he couldn't stop touching her face. "Denounce me, and use your lovely, pure magick to break anything false that may lie here and we shall see what is real and what is illusion."

It was then that the bitter laughter started.

And nothing he said could make her stop. But eventually the bitter laughter turned into tears and she curled against him and wept.

"The magick is gone."

Jaren stared at her sleeping figure and tried to come to grips with what Aryn had told him. Such an act would have surely driven most, if not all, of the kin truly insane. Or just simply killed them. Magick was part of their makeup, part of what they were inside, like their skin color, their hair, their blood. And she had taken it out. It had been a sheer act of desperation. De Asir knew what to do against a soul eater. Tyriel did not. A lone elf did not. But lone elves rarely ventured out into the mortal realms.

And the mages who knew how to work such magick—only a few had ever existed. 'Twas insanity.

'Twas also one of the most sincere, truest acts of heroism he had ever seen in all his years. Men like this jackal were the reason the elves lived in secret. If he had found their stronghold, or discovered the gypsies' haunts, the world would be short many saviors. But she was hollow inside now.

"If you let her see the pity in your eyes, do you really think that is going to help?" Aryn asked quietly as he moved past the assassin to settle down on the ground beside Tyriel. He arranged his bedroll and shucked his jerkin before turning to face the elf. "She will not want or need your pity."

"I cannot help that I pity her."

"Pity her all you wish. But she doesn't have to see it all over your face." Aryn moved his eyes to where she lay sleeping, her sleep fitful, but deep, thanks to a restorative brew Jaren had concocted. Aryn had fed it to her, spoonful by spoonful, and now it was helping her rest and further heal by replacing the stores that had been drained dry during her captivity. It would take more than just one bowl of it—more like a vat, or several of them.

But it was a start.

"We need to do more than this—but is she strong enough to move?" Aryn didn't know enough about an elf's physiology to make this choice. If she was too weak, and they moved her, then she would die.

Jaren moved one broad shoulder absently, then rubbed his temple. "I think we must try. She cannot stay out here. I would ask the Healer." He nodded his head to the stallion that never strayed too far from the gypsy-elf's side.

The Healer, eh? With a curve of his lips, Aryn made his way to the stallion in silence, his booted feet making little noise over the grassy terrain. But Kilidare heard him all the same and turned dark, turbulent eyes his way.

"She sleeps. Too much. All the time."

That powerful, intelligent voice that boomed into his mind would never cease to amaze him. Aryn lowered himself to his heels by the stallion, the leather of his breeches stretching tightly across powerful, muscled thighs, molding to a firm, muscled ass as he studied Tyriel's pale face, tormented even in sleep.

"I know, Kilidare. We need to take her back to Averne, to her father's people in Eivisa but we aren't sure if it's safe to move her. The elf suggests we ask the Healer." Aryn dipped his head in acknowledgment to Kilidare and lifted a brow, waiting for an answer, the wind blowing his hair around his face, into his eyes.

Kilidare's ears flicked. He arched his head around and rubbed his velvety nose against Tyriel's cheek, her neck. *"Averne. Yes. Needs her people's Healer, her home. And you. Heart hurts for you."*

Kilidare insisted he take them into Averne, mounted on his back. Jaren whispered secrets into Bel's ear and said obliquely, "Your mortal mount will find his way into Averne. I have shown him the way. It will take him a while, though not as long since he travels without weight."

And now Aryn was atop an elvish stallion, holding a weak and weary half-elf in his strong arms as Jaren lengthened the straps to accommodate his longer legs.

Aryn held her body cupped in the cradle of his thighs and shuddered, breathing the scent of her hair and body, closing his free hand into a fist and praying for strength. She didn't need this from his body right now. And even as he was thinking it, she felt him, and stiffened. Resting his hand on her hip, he lowered his mouth and whispered in her ear, "Shhh. You're safe—you know I would never hurt you, don't you?"

"Yes," she said weakly. And one hand came up and closed over his lightly.

"I've gone mad, this past year without you. You cannot know how mad. And when I discovered you were in danger, I was ready to tear all of Ithyrian apart to find you. But you're safe with me, I swear it." He nuzzled the black curls atop her head, soft and sweet-smelling once more, but still dull and lifeless from so much starvation.

"To Averne, where you will heal, become strong and healthy." Jaren lifted his solemn eyes to his Princess and then turned away and mounted his own elvish steed, a tall, willowy stallion, golden, with a white mane, and blue eyes, a sharp contrast to his dark hair and dark clothes. He took off at a ground-eating run, with Kilidare in his wake. Aryn's eyes widened, one hand gripped the reins tightly and the other held firmly to Tyriel's waist, her tight little ass pressed snug against his cock.

He stifled a groan in his throat and chanced a glance at the ground, watching it blur beneath the stallion's feet. Kilidare moved like the very wind itself. But so smooth, like rain sliding down a rock...or...or like the caress of her fingers on the back of his hand. Ahhh...what was he doing?

Her head shifted into the hollow just below his neck, and her fingers continued to absently play over the back of his hand. And her other hand went to his thigh. Just resting there. Lightly. Her body moved easily with Kilidare's, even as weak as she was, and with Aryn holding her slight weight atop the mount, she didn't have to do anything with her hands, or her attention.

What is she thinking about? Aryn's thoughts were more to himself, but Irian's answer didn't really come as a surprise.

"Not one thing. She isna thinkin' at all, about anything. She canna think right now, not much." Irian's voice was full of weariness and pain. *"Your body, your touch, your presence, brings her comfort."*

So Aryn withstood the torture of her hands moving so silkily on his body, while his cock throbbed and ached like a bad tooth, as they rode nearly until dark, stopping only when Kilidare insisted that Tyriel needed a break.

As Jaren moved into the woods to fetch more of the mushrooms and foliage needed for making her brew, Tyriel stood staring up at the star-studded sky with lost, lonesome eyes. She was so awfully quiet, even for her. Things were broken inside her, and she wasn't quite certain how to handle it.

Two large warm hands landed on her shoulders. With a sigh, she leaned back against Aryn's hard, firm body. She felt him stiffen, and then relax as his arms came around her, cuddling around her waist and holding her firmly against him as he nuzzled his face against her neck, pressing a gentle kiss to her mouth. "I was a fool to leave the inn alone. I knew there was darkness, even without Irian's warning," she whispered softly. "I damn near died, but I endangered all my people, others as well."

"Hush." Aryn lifted his lips from her neck and kissed her temple gently. "Look…" He lifted one hand, and a gently glowing orb, filled with a swirling mist that cleared to reveal two figures, one that shimmered and wore the ancient garb of a long-dead warrior enchanter. Irian, as he argued with Aryn, to tell Tyriel. "He wanted me to tell you what is in my heart, what has been in my heart for years. You did not hear all."

"Danger and darkness wait, and all for her."

Like a play, it showed Aryn rising from his bedroll, weary, sleepless, frustrated. Hungry. Tyriel came to that conclusion on her own, after he kept sending her sleeping form long, narrow glances. He slid his hands to her hips and lowered his lips to her ear and whispered, "Aye. Hungry. For you."

The orb showed him pacing far away from camp to avoid disturbing his partner, and Irian shimmering out of his resting place, and the words that were spoken between them.

Tyriel and Aryn watched the orb as Aryn turned and met the eyes of the long-dead enchanter. "Tyriel is in danger?" he asked doubtfully. "She can handle any blasted thing that comes her way."

"Not this time. Turn back, before she is lost to you." Irian's voice was like a deep, rolling rumble that both of them heard quite clearly.

"Why do you insist on talking like the woman belongs to me?" Aryn growled, advancing on Irian. "She is not mine. Not ours."

"She could be yours. Take her. Keep her, love her." Irian's eyes were dark and haunted, tormented it seemed, by more than he had wanted to tell Aryn. What secrets haunted the enchanter? What had led him to trap his soul inside a metal casing, enchained for millennia?

In the orb, the echoes from the past played on. "Love her? Her? Keep her?" Aryn sputtered, but Tyriel was almost afraid to believe what her eyes told her. What her heart was telling her—it just didn't seem possible. For what she saw on his face—loving her, keeping her, was just what he wanted, not something foolish and repulsive as she had thought all those months ago.

Irian cocked his head, studying Aryn with eyes that were dark with frustration. "Aye. The girl loves you, madly. The need is an ache in her belly to be with you, feel you."

"You'd tell me any damn thing it took if you thought it would get me to climb atop her and fuck her," Aryn growled. They could see the strain there, but it was evident as well, just how much he wanted to do exactly as the enchanter wished. His eyes were dark and burning with his own hunger, a love he had never shown, and refused to let out. "She is not for me. I am not for her. We are partners, nothing more. We will never be more."

"You deny that she is in your heart. You will admit you want her, because wanting a woman is easy," Irian said softly. "You want to touch her, taste her, fuck her, love her. Do it."

"No. If I need a woman, want a woman, I'll find a fucking whore in Ifteril." And through the orb's enchantment his own thoughts were loud and clear as well, his emotions, how his body felt, it all filled and pulsed through them — how his cock throbbed against his belly, how his heart ached with need for her and how all he wanted, all, was lying in her bedroll, not far away. *Yes! All I want lies there. All.*

Her body shuddered in his arms. That hunger, that need, all focused on her. That yearning, so very similar to her own — was it real?

"I was more foolish than you," he murmured softly, lowering his head to kiss her mass of curls. "By far. If I had listened to my heart, my soul, even my companion, none of this would have happened. I need to beg your forgiveness, but I do not feel I have that right after how you have suffered."

Slowly, almost afraid to look, she turned and stared up into his eyes.

Tyriel saw a reflection of what she felt deep inside her heart—a deep, burning need that was etched forever on her soul, for this one man, for all of eternity. "Why did you not tell me?" she whispered in a voice thick with tears, her throat tight, her chest burning and aching.

He caressed one gentle hand over the curve of one ear. "Tyriel, you are the beautiful daughter of an elvish Prince, a royal Princess of the kin. The daughter of gypsy chieftains, the offspring of the most valiant and proud people this world will ever know. And you are a creature of magick who will walk this world for centuries to come. I expected I would die within decades. Why wish such grief upon you?"

A sob rose and built in her chest. "I didn't care–I don't. I just wanted..." Her voice trailed off as he covered her lips with two gentle fingers, his dark sapphire eyes staring into hers.

"I cared. I could not bear the thought of you suffering any pain for me." Then Aryn's eyes lowered, closing briefly before they lifted, revealing a swirling morass of blue glowing lights. "But something inside of me is changing. Irian has seen to that. I do not yet know if I will live the length of time an elf lives. But I will not fade away and leave you alone in a handful of years either."

Tyriel gasped as she placed one hand on his chest and felt the throb of power inside him. Though her magick was gone, she could still feel it, still sense it. The power that ebbed and flowed in him was new. Burning bright and powerful—and enough to sustain him for centuries. "By the Blood, where did this come from?" Her fingers flexed against the gleaming pale wall of carved muscle there and she shuddered as an unwelcome flood of need started to pulse inside her.

Unwelcome...her body was still too afraid, she couldn't handle those desires yet.

"Irian. His magick is forcing its way completely inside me. Before long, it will all be there." Aryn forced his eyes to open wider and he stared into hers, reveling in the heavy, sexual feel of the magick, and the feel of her hand on his bare skin.

But her face was dark and troubled.

"And when all of his magick is there, what of Irian?"

* * * * *

Irian drifted.

He let the memories pull him back, centuries and centuries, until he was once more staring into dark sloe-eyes as he thrust deep within a woman's body, her pussy gripping his cock greedily while she screamed out his name.

Her name had been Fael and he had loved her with all his heart and soul, but he had never told her of his love.

She had been mortal, and ungifted, and he wouldn't bind himself to a woman who would die before he even aged.

But she had died in a raider's attack within a season after he turned her away. She had refused his offer of *sueta*, a lover and companion, for a time, to a magick maker. She had accepted an offering from a Jiupsu warrior in another clan many weeks away. They had been traveling to their home when the raiders attacked.

She had been young, lovely, and the raiders hadn't killed her or the other young women like her. Which was their ultimate downfall. Too many of the women were magicked and they sent up cries even as they fought off their rapists.

By the time Irian found her, her spirit had been broken, her body bruised, torn and bleeding inside, death slowly laying its hold over her.

He had robbed them of decades together...and now she had only moments, for her spirit was drifting further and further away as she stared into his eyes, smiling. "Irian, my handsome brave warrior...did you fight well?"

"Fael, I'm sorry..."

"Shh, you did not do this to me. I did, with my pride. I could have stayed...persuaded you otherwise..."

"So sorry..." and tears fell down his face. "I love you, my lovely lady, beautiful, strong woman."

"My handsome warrior, I love you as well. I have always loved you and always will. We will meet again. Our souls are one, they belong together..." Her eyes went dark and she was gone.

And then he was on the cliff, as a massive fire raged higher and higher. Asrel was primed for the ritual, the hilt wedged between two huge rocks, strong enough to take his weight. *Until all the wrongs are righted...* He lifted his eyes skyward, searching for the star that must hold Fael's soul. *Our souls will never be together, for I cost an innocent her life. But I cannot meet the dark one, even him, with this taint on my soul.*

Such a powerful enchantment never had he worked. The circle of salt was as thick in width as his thigh, and the diameter was easily the span of a lodge tent. He slashed his wrist deeply with a magicked knife, one that would keep his own enchanted body from healing itself as he paced the blood circle thrice.

Until the wrongs are righted, inside the sword I dwell.

And inside the circle of salt and blood he rammed his body home on the blade.

As his body died, his soul was trapped inside the sword.

He drifted on, but this time to a place he had not traversed before. And to a face he had not seen in all the millennia that he had walked the earth—not since that night had he seen her outside of his memories.

"Fael..." he whispered hoarsely.

"Irian." Her husky, warm voice stroked over him like a satin caress and her inky-black curls fell over his body as she leaned down to kiss his stunned face. "Love, why must you torment yourself? Have you not chained yourself to your own guilt long enough?"

"Fael? Are you really here?"

She smiled and lifted his hands to her face. "I am really here, love. Lover. My heart," she crooned in the Jiupsu. "So many years you have walked this earth, buried inside a metal body, carrying out vengeance for people you know not, with your broken heart and your aching loneliness. Let it go...rest."

All around them a gentle silvery light glowed and pulsed, and a soft wind played with their hair.

"'I cannot change the enchantment. Until all is done, until all wrongs are righted —"

Her lips, soft, warm, sweet as cynaber wine, covered his and Irian groaned roughly, burying his hands in her hair and crushing her tightly to him. She whispered softly, "The only wrongs are in your heart. Let them go...and come to me. Find me. I long for you..."

Irian was jerked into awareness.

It was morning and they were heading out.

"Come to me...I long for you."

Fael. Sweet Fael. Ahh, so long. Is it possible? Was it possible that after this was all done, he could be with her?

He settled his presence around Tyriel, feeling her weariness, her fear, and then her acceptance of his presence. Her gratitude.

First, the elf. He had failed one woman he loved. He would not fail another. But once he knew she was safe, that she would be well — then he would seek out Fael.

And see.

Chapter Twelve

The mountains of Eivisa rose tall and majestic in the air. Spiraling into the sky, dipping low to give way to deep, mysterious valleys where magickal creatures flitted about. The wards on the land made Aryn itch as they crossed over, as Jaren had warned, but once he simply stood and absorbed it, the land seemed to almost open and accept him, and it rejoiced in his burden. It rejoiced until it detected her injuries, and then the mountains trembled and shook, the skies darkened, and the wind howled furiously through the trees.

"My lord Prince knows she is coming, and he knows now that she is not well," Jaren said flatly.

"What in the hell was that?" Aryn asked as the storm slowly blew itself out.

"Me." Tyriel's head fell back against Aryn's shoulder and she snuggled closer, achingly cold. He wrapped his cloak more firmly around her and secured her against his body with his forearm. "It reacts to what is inside. And I am a storm."

Jaren's face went grim. "It will be an earthquake once my Lord Prince sees you."

"Da has better control than that."

No. He did not.

But he had received them in an iron chamber, where his emotions could not leak to the world outside. Tyriel's passing into the land had filled him with foreboding and he dared not rush out to meet them.

His wife, Alys, waited with him, clad in working leather of white, her hair braided away from her face, a simple golden coronet at her brow the only marking of her rank as they moved into the chamber, awaiting the arrival of the long missing princess. The iron walls were swathed with silks to dull the harming effects on the kin, and well-padded with heavy carpeting, so that none of the blasted metal showed. This room was solely used to protect the kingdom. Or to block spying eyes—no Fae creature could possibly trespass in any way in this room. Not by hiding, and not by craft.

Only a magick bearer of great means could tolerate this room for more than mere minutes. And none could tolerate it for hours on end, except Tyriel.

And since the room was locked by a true iron lock that couldn't be opened with magick, hiding inside it was out of the question.

And using mind magick to peek inside was impossible, since the metal blocked all Fae magick.

Except for Tyriel's.

Surely she could have reached out to him by now.

"Why does she not touch me?" Josah said roughly, dragging a long-fingered, slim hand through his waist-length red hair. "What troubles the child?"

"Josah. Have a care, show some patience. We know not where she has been, or what has happened to her all these months. She is coming, she lives. We can handle all, knowing that."

No. Not all, Josah thought as a tall, broad-shouldered mortal carried his daughter through the door some time later. His eyes were grim, his face stoic, but it softened with love as he gazed down at the woman in his arms.

But it wasn't Tyriel. Was it?

The bright, glowing magick that had filled his child from birth was missing.

But the dark eyes that turned to face him were those of his daughter. And those eyes filled with tears, and her mouth trembled, like it had when she had hurt herself as a youngling, though she tried so very hard to be brave.

"Da..."

"Her magick is gone."

"How does an elf survive without it?" Josah whispered to Alys some time later as she entered their chambers, her body aching and weary.

Her mind was troubled, very troubled. The girl had suffered too many torments, and she could not tell her father all of them, and had not wanted him told. And he would want to know. Her mouth quirked. At least she had the Healer's vow to fall upon when her liege lord issued a direct order.

"If she was wholly elvin, she would not have survived. The metal alone would have killed her. The killing of her own magick would have killed her. But both—'twas an act of desperation and courage the likes of which I've never heard," Alys murmured, nestling against his side. "Her man watches over her so fiercely. Elvish magick is too distracting to healing magick, but his augmented mine and he calms her so—speaking soothingly, and distracting her gently while I work.

"But he watches me with those dark, probing eyes, eyes like the sapphires we find in our mines, and I know that I must not fail her, or him," Alys murmured. "And another…soul. I feel another soul within, almost battling for supremacy, one that watches me all the same, that guards and protects her manically."

"What of my daughter?"

Alys closed her lavender eyes. Her silvery hair fell down to cover her face as she buried her eyes against his chest. "I have done all I can. The healing of her body has already started. Her soul will be healed by home, and her lover. But the magick…I do not know."

Tyriel felt so empty inside. The painful, vicious aches from so many beatings was gone, thanks to Alys' wondrous healing, and the muffled thudding inside her had finally died away as the poison from the iron was leeched from her system.

But it was more than that, beyond that.

The magick…

Its loss left something torn open inside her.

Hot tears seeped out from under her lids as she lay on the silken bed where she had slept for so many years, safe and sound under her father's roof. If only she had never left here—no. No, she would not unwish her life.

"A brave lass you've always been," Irian whispered as he shimmered into view, kneeling beside her bed. Aryn's arm tightened around her waist, making her more aware of his presence as he slid closer to wakefulness. She felt the brush of Irian's hand across her brow as he smoothed her tumbled hair out of her face. *"I canna promise that all things will be well, but I can promise that I'll do all in my power to make it so, sweet little elf, lovely lady of Jiupsu,"* he murmured, his raw silk voice rasping over her shredded

nerves like a gentle caress, soothing her, stroking her, calming her battered soul. *"A warrior to sing and dance…now sleep…"*

And oddly enough, she did, sliding into slumber as Aryn slid out, opening his blue eyes and meeting Irian's over the limp sprawl of her body.

"The Healer tells me her body will recover." A sour chuckle fell from his lips and his head fell back. His eyes roamed over the domed ceiling and he studied the swirls of paint there, as if searching for an answer. "Her body. What of her heart? Her soul? What of Tyriel, Irian? Will Tyriel recover? Will I ever again look into her eyes and see laughter dancing there?"

The enchanter sighed, a deep echoing sound that rippled through the chamber. *"I canna say. She took more torture and abuse than any woman should have to endure. It would break most. She's not yet broken, but she is close. Aryn, my friend, my brother, hold tight to her."*

A breath of a moment passed, and the enchanter was gone.

When Irian opened his eyes next, he was in the ether plane, studying himself. In all the years he had walked the world, he had amassed great resources of strength. So much power—would it be enough?

He stripped away the walls that separated Tyriel from her own magick. Walls—that was all it was. *Eh, it didna matter truly, that she had shoved the power outside her body now, did it?* He could bring it to her easily enough. She had not put it out, she had blocked it away, and the fire had nigh burnt out. She was too powerful a creature to completely extinguish it. But she almost had, almost.

Aryn lay sleeping against her back and Irian smiled as he studied the swordsman. *A good friend you were, mortal. A good friend.* Then he sighed and lowered himself to settle down on the ground, as a soft, familiar hum started to sound in the distance.

Fael...she was waiting.

As he reached for the blade and salt, the music of her voice grew louder, and Irian smiled.

Tyriel felt his hands on her body, felt a hot, itching burning deep inside her. She turned her face and caught his mouth with hers, hungrily, avidly pushing her tongue into his mouth, sobbing as he slid his hands under her shirt and sought out her breasts, plumping up the curves and pinching her nipples until they stood hard and erect, stabbing into his palms.

A rumbling, hoarse groan sounded against her throat as Aryn tore his mouth from hers, kissing his way down her neck, her collarbone, until he could fasten his lips around the peak of one breast, tugging sharply with his teeth before suckling deep, laving it with his tongue as she buried her fingers in his hair and held his head tight against her.

Rainbows blossomed behind her eyes as she rocked her hips upward, caressing the firm heavy girth of his cock beneath the loose silken trousers he had donned before climbing into bed. She whimpered low under her breath and opened her eyes just a little, staring down at the blond head at her breast, his silky hair spilling over her body, the tip of one reddened nipple peeking through the strands as he lifted his head to stare at her with slumberous eyes.

Tyriel raked her nails down his chest, staring at him greedily before meeting his sleep-dazed eyes with her own. He smiled slightly before crushing her beneath him, trailing the tips of his fingers over the silvery mark of the demon-scar that started under her breast and crossed over her torso. "Not ready to wake up yet," he murmured against her neck.

"Hmm." No dream…

But if he was happier to think they were dreaming, she would do nothing to change that. Her nipples stabbed hotly into his chest and she arched her hips against his, cradling his sex between her thighs as she spread her legs and whimpered. He started to rock against her, riding her with short, subtle little thrusts that stroked right against the bud of her clit.

"Such a hot, sweet little thing." The words were murmured against her neck as Aryn started to move his way down her body, pressing kisses first to her neck, then her breastbone, her belly, her navel, and then he was stabbing at her pulsating clit with his tongue as he pumped two fingers into and out of her weeping cleft. She rocked her hips up, taking him as deeply as she could, sobbing against the back of her hand.

A vicious memory, the backlash of brutal angry hands started to invade and the gentle brush of Irian's mind slid into hers *"…not here…they've no place here…"*and then she was lost again as Aryn spread the lips of her sex open and plunged his tongue inside her, greedily lapping at her swollen, slick flesh, a greedy hungry sound rumbling out of him just as she went screaming into climax.

It was the sound of her scream that woke him. "Oh, please, Aryn, yes!" That glorious, gasping scream, the tang of her cream on his tongue, the feel of her naked mound against his mouth and lips as he pushed up to stare at her, head befuddled with sleep, and his cock aching and raging with the need to crawl up her lithe body and bury himself inside her and hear her scream out his name, only his name...

Her hands fisted in the silken skeins of his hair, and she tugged, pulling him up. *"Mevas a ve."* Love me. She pressed her mouth to his, rubbing her hips frantically against his, the slick wet folds of her cleft opening eagerly for him.

Aryn pressed his brow to hers as he gasped for air. "Tyriel, damn it, you're not ready for this—"

"Aryn, please! I've been ready for years," she pleaded, her eyes gleaming wet with tears.

He growled out her name as he reached between them for the drawstring at his waist, the silken trousers slithered down his hips and his cock sprang free, ruddy, red and swollen, the tip gleaming with moisture as he lowered himself atop her. "Bloody hell, you don't know how long I've wanted this. Me...me." His breath brushed her face in a soft caress of air as he took his cock in hand and shifted between her thighs, spreading her legs wider, opening her for him.

"Years, years," he crooned as he pushed the first inch inside the silky tight embrace of her pussy, clenching his teeth and shuddering as she arched up against him, taking another two inches inside with the motion. "I know he's taken you with my body, and part of me hates him for it. This time is mine."

And every time hereafter.

Irian's voice echoed as magick exploded in the room and through their bodies, arching Aryn's back, thrusting his cock, deep, deep inside her cleft. She screamed out his name and arched her hips up, taking him as deeply inside her as she could. Heat exploded through every last nerve ending inside her, while the walls fell away and the magick exploded back through her body, behind her eyelids and outside her, falling from her lips in a glorious peal of sound as Aryn pulled out and surged back inside her. The wet snug clasp of her sheath made him grit his teeth as she shrieked and clawed her nails down his arms.

Hot molten little licks of magick caressed her belly, her clit, her nipples as Aryn slid his hands down her back and sides, cupping her ass and lifting her harder against him. Pulling her against him, he moved against the bundled nerves of her clit each time he drove his cock inside her.

The muscles in his chest and belly worked and played, gleaming under a fine coat of sweat. He shifted, tossing his hair over one shoulder so that he could cup her breast in his hand, tweaking the nipple between his thumb and forefinger before lowering his head and catching it between his teeth and pulling on it until she was sobbing and gasping for breath. "I love you," Aryn whispered softly, pressing his mouth to her ear. "Always, forever."

Running his hand down her ass, he breached the seam there, probing the rosette until it opened the smallest bit and he could enter with the tip of his finger. She climaxed around his rigid cock with a broken scream, bracing her hands against his shoulders and working herself against his cock, her swollen, slick tissues hugging it tightly. The beaded, red buds of her nipples stabbed into his chest and Aryn groaned. Brilliant starbursts of light broke overhead while the slick, satin tissues of her pussy contracted around him, milking him.

He rose up on his hands, plundering her deeper, harder, feeling her tighten around him even further, listening as she started to scream and pant yet again. Her hands settled around his waist and Aryn tossed his sweaty hair out of his eyes, staring down into her dark-brown gaze, at her flushed face, seeing the sparkle of life returning there.

"Come...come for me, let me feel it," he purred, pulling out of her and flipping her onto her hands and knees, his cock wet and ruddy as he pushed into her from behind. He trailed his hands down her back, his eyes glowing faintly in the dimness of the room. They lingered on her gleaming golden skin, her tousled black curls and the tight curve of her ass. Pulling her snug against his pelvis, he pushed back into her, canting her hips down so that he passed low over the bundled bed of nerves buried deep inside her.

She sobbed out his name, quivering as he stroked his hands over her ass, smacking one flank lightly before pulling her back against him. "Come..." He felt the rushing, whirling wind dancing over his skin, blowing his hair back from his face as the magick broke over her, sparkling billowing streams of lights breaking from her body as she rushed closer to climax.

He slid his hand around and pinched her clit. She climaxed around his cock, into his hand with a scream, and Aryn went rigid, setting his teeth into her shoulder and biting down, marking her. Wild magick flooded the room as his cock jerked and he pumped her full of hot, milky seed, filling her with short hard shafts until she had emptied him dry, while she screamed out his name, contracting around him and sobbing.

Tyriel opened her eyes early the next morning. Her body ached from good, hard sex.

But more…when she opened her eyes, she saw colors and shapes and mists that hadn't been there when she had gone to bed that past night. She closed her eyes, certain she was dreaming, but the afterimages remained there, even with her lids closed, burning brightly, lingering. Slowly, she sat up, the blankets falling to her waist, her nipples tightening in the cool morning air as she looked around the room.

Her eyes fell on Aryn's long, pale body, muscled and gleaming like it was carved from alabaster. Touching her tongue to her lips nervously, she reached out and touched a trembling hand to his hip, jerking it back suddenly when the hot, rush of magick under his skin threatened to burn her.

"Aye, if that's no' a pretty sight so early in the morn,'" a low, husky voice murmured. It slid around her body like a caress as Aryn's eyes slowly opened. He sat up slowly as Irian's form shimmered into view.

His form was more transparent than normal, and his eyes were dark with regret, grief, and exhaustion.

How could a ghost look so tired? Tyriel studied his weary face as he moved closer and knelt beside the bed, staring up at her with a look of adoration on his face.

"Ever it was you, lovely lady," Irian murmured softly, his voice low and distant. *"I wanted, badly, ah, so badly, to be with you. I envied the swordsman every breath he took, I envied him. But now, I am tired. I go to my rest. The wrongs are righted."*

"What wrongs?" Tyriel reached out and threaded her hand through Irian's hair as Aryn moved up behind her, aligning his hard, warm body with hers, cupping her body with the line of his. Tyriel stroked her hand through the enchanter's dark curls; the sadness, the sheer exhaustion in his eyes, pulling at her heart. "I know you feel you have some great wrong to atone for, but I find it hard to believe a man as noble as you—"

"Noble? I? Not a noble man, was I, lovely lady. Not then. And not now. I took a sweet, lovely virgin to my bed, but refused to wed her because she wasna gifted, and she died thinkin' I didna love her," Irian growled, jerking away from her tenderly stroking hand. He shot to his feet and paced the room in long angry strides. *"And in my cowardice, did I face the penance I should have at the end of my natural life? No. I prolonged it, in a metal casing, hoping to right the many wrongs a selfish, self-centered, arrogant enchanter did...and caused many more. Forcing my will on others, time after time again."*

"And you." He turned hot, hungry eyes to the couple on the bed, staring at Tyriel with blind need. *"Ahhh, you. Lovely, wild little elf. You. I wanted you like I had wanted none other since Fael. And I used whatever means I had to take you, and you call me a noble man."*

"Even noble men make mistakes, and do the wrong thing. She called you noble, Irian, not a bleeding Saint," Aryn said gruffly, wrapping his arms around Tyriel, holding her tightly against him. Burning jealousy ate at him. How many times had Irian touched her, using his body? How many?

"How many? Shall I tell him, elf? As he tries to tell me that noble men make mistakes?" Irian glided back over them, smirking angrily at them.

"Two nights, Aryn. Only two, in five long years. Do not let him anger you," Tyriel said huskily. "He is being terribly evil today for some reason and I know not why. But do not let him anger you."

"Evil?" Irian's tired laugh filled the room and his eyes, filled with a bittersweet yearning, and an odd gleam,

something that looked to her like hope, landed on Tyriel's face. *"Am I feeling evil, love? No. Just very bitter. I was told that I would see her, and I am hopin' she didna lie t' me. I'm makin' my goodbyes t' you, pretty elf. And t' you, brother of my soul. I shouldna be makin' it such a bitter moment."*

"Your time here is done, isn't it?" Tyriel asked as Aryn was still absorbing what the enchanter was saying.

With narrowed eyes, Aryn shook his head. "He's playing some fool trick, Tyriel. I'm not likely to be rid of him that easily."

"Don't, Aryn." She brushed her fingers down his hand before untangling herself from his arms. "He is not playing a fool trick. He is well and truly leaving." Staring into those black eyes, she reached out, cupping his face in her hands, opening her mind, her heart. The words that fell from her lips came from someplace outside of her — and it shook the enchanter to the core. "She waits for you...but not in the ether planes. Your lives are yet to be lived."

His hands, transparent, yet solid to the touch, closed around her wrists, as he rasped out, *"What say you? Where is Fael?"*

An ethereal smile curved Tyriel's lips. "Waiting...shouldn't you go and find her?" Then she shook her head and the dazed look left her, leaving behind an aching sadness. "I owe you, so much. I've a part of me back, and it's because of you, I know it."

Irian rose, pausing to press a tender kiss to her brow. *"There was a wall blocking it — I merely tore it down, lovely lady of the Jiupsu. Such a warrior, you are. Sing and dance...and remember me."* He straightened and turned burning, intense eyes on Aryn, pinning the swordsman with a brief, flitting smile. *"Ever a true friend ye've been to me, swordsman.*

I wish I could say I have been as true a friend t' you as you were t' me. But a gift I give t' ye… What powers I had in life, are yours. And a bloody good enchanter I was. Taught you the best I could — a true teacher you must find, a flesh and blood one. A long, long life you've to live with your lovely elf. And a strong blade, enchanted still, just no longer ensouled."

Wrapping his arm around Tyriel's narrow, naked waist, he nodded. The many words he needed to voice were trapped in his throat. But he could see that the enchanter understood — it was there in the vast darkness of those black eyes. "Go and find your lady, Irian. You've been waiting for thousands of years — don't wait any longer," he said gruffly.

A brilliant, blinding flash of a grin lit Irian's face, and a splash of light filled the room, and his transparent form was swallowed by a gleaming star-washed sky that exploded into brilliant starbursts, so bright it hurt their eyes.

When it faded, he was gone, leaving an emptiness inside Aryn. Tyriel brushed tears away from her dusky cheeks before cuddling against her lover. "He gave it up for me." Her voice was low and hushed as she nuzzled his chest with her cheek. "I know my powers, the feel and the scent of them. These are mine, well enough, but he didn't just tear down a wall. He went and found them, brought them back for me."

Aryn smiled in answer, unable to speak just yet. He felt a little too empty. Like the other half of him was missing.

But as Tyriel shifted and squirmed on his lap, pressing her damp cheek to his, his cock twitched, and the scent of her filled his head. Tumbling her to her back, he stared down at her. "Umm…he was right…a very pretty sight so early in the morn," he mused, stroking her hair away from her flushed face, staring into her topaz eyes. The blue stone in his ear winked in the morning light as he lowered his mouth to kiss her gently, licking away the tear tracks before resting his brow against hers. "My heart has been yours almost from the first. I was a fool not to let you know, whatever my reasons were."

Her arms, seemingly still so weak and frail, slid around his neck and held him tight. A low husky laugh fell from her lips, caressing his ear. "Aye, a bloody fool. So many nights you cost us, Aryn of Olsted."

With a mischievous twinkle gleaming in her slanted eyes, she smiled up at him. "It's going to take me a bit of time to get back to my old self. But you know...you owe me. I think you should pay me back with lots of slavish devotion, lots of time, spent on your knees, kissing and pleading for my forgiveness."

Aryn leaned down and covered that smiling mouth with his, so glad to have her there, back in his arms. Pushing his tongue into her mouth, swallowing her taste down with greed, he pressed his knee between her thighs and mounted her, driving his engorged cock into her wet, waiting pussy, circling his thumb around her clit.

She was panting and clutching at his shoulders, the silky fit of her sheath squeezing down around his cock until his eyes were crossing at the pleasure of it. Tearing his mouth away from hers, he whispered huskily into her ear, "I'm your slave."

Hooking her ankles around his waist, Tyriel giggled. "Good." Arching her head back, her black curls falling like a cloak around her, she hurtled into climax with a moan. The muscles in her vagina clutched and contracted around his thrusting flesh as she shuddered and screamed out his name. At the sound, his cock jerked and he jetted his milky seed deep inside her.

Aryn's rigid body went lax and he slowly fell against her, moving down and resting his head low on her belly.

Her fingers laced through his hair and he sighed. "I love you..." Her murmured whisper echoed through his mind as she slid into sleep. Aryn waited until her soft sighs filled the room before he moved and wrapped his arm around her, stroking his hand up and down her arm, staring at her exotic, dusky face.

"Love you, wild little elf."

Epilogue

Irian followed the music.

Fael...

He could hear her, laughing playfully, tauntingly, teasingly...as he drifted. He had no form any longer, no body, not Aryn's, not the steel casing of Asrel's, not the borrowed body of another bearer. None.

With a sudden, tearing jerk, he was ripped from the drifting and thrown into another form, small, tiny, awkward...bright lights...cold...and harsh voices. No memories, no thoughts...nothing.

Just the music...and the echo of a woman's laughter.

The following is an excerpt from:

COMING IN LAST

COMING IN LAST

"So what's eating you?"

Sliding Mick a glance, Jamie lifted his shoulders in a disinterested shrug and said, "Not much." Flipping through the file on his desk, he skimmed the account information they had received, and cursed mildly the sense of family obligation that had him agreeing to drive two hours south and stay there, for heaven only knows how long.

Of course, it wasn't like he had anything more interesting to do at the time.

"You know, you've had that same damn look on your face for about the past six months, like nothing on this earth can hold your attention for longer than five minutes."

Flashing Mick a grin, Jamie said, "Well, anything having to do with your ugly mug is gonna bore me senseless in five seconds. What's your point?"

"Just wondering when you're gonna snap out of this, that's all." Mick shrugged, lifting his shoulders as he sipped from his coffee before flipping a page and studying the next. "You know, this is really a waste of time. Time and money—his money, our time."

"His money. He can afford us. And this was slick, slick and pat. There may well be more missing than what is showing," Jamie mused, eyeing the accounts.

"There is that," Mick said with a nod. "So when are you gonna snap out of it?"

"Snap out of what?"

"This funk."

Jamie sighed. "Mick, I'm bored. Okay? Just bored." He laughed, recalling the scene with Erin from the previous weekend. "I can think about business while I'm getting a blowjob, and a damn good one. Tell me what in the hell the problem is here?"

"You need to let me have the woman while you get your head examined?" Mick offered blandly.

Jamie rose, the tailored suit falling into place over his gun as he strode over to the window and stood staring out into the clear summer day. "Something is just…missing, Mick. I'm bored with all of this. Everything. All of it. Not the business, but my life. Erin was just the exact same as every other woman I'd gone out with before her. And the next one will be just like her."

* * * * *

There was something about a woman surrounded by kids, Jamie mused. Some guys tended to be put off by the sight, but Jamie loved it—loved watching women as they held and rocked, soothed and played with children.

Her laugh floated above the higher-pitched laughter of the kids as she unlocked the pudgy little arms from her leg and lifted the baby. Settling him on her hip, she answered one question after another as she wove her way through the maze of toys and games already spilled out on the floor.

The high-pitched peals of laughter and the squeak of excited voices had his head pounding again. Wincing, Jamie pressed his hand gingerly to his throbbing temple, wishing for a bit of peace and quiet. Hell, he had planned on coming down here with a feigned injury, not a real one.

Right before he could open his mouth, she stopped mid-stride and turned her head, meeting his eyes across the room. Light reflected off her glasses, keeping him from seeing her eyes. She turned her head and the chunky teenager took the baby from her.

"Hello."

Squinting against the bright light, cursing the throbbing in his head, he managed to growl out, "Hi."

"Looks like you bumped your head," she said. Without asking, she laid one hand on his arm and guided him around the perimeter of the room, sidestepping toys and toddlers with ease. "The clinic is right over here."

Moments later, laying flat on his back, eyes closed against the harsh glare of light, Jamie mumbled around the thermometer, "Is all this really necessary?"

"Company policy," she replied as she wrapped a blood pressure cuff around his arm. Competent, quick hands checked his vitals while Jamie lay there waiting for the Motrin he'd taken to kick in. Strong, cool, slender fingers wrapped around his wrist. It was just the pain that caused his pulse to race, Jamie told himself.

A subtle scent wafted over to taunt him. God, she smelled good.

Through the fringe of his lashes, he watched as she rose from kneeling on the floor and smoothed down the plain, simple white utilitarian scrubs she wore. As she turned away, his eyes locked on the long red braid that hung between her shoulder blades. Her hips swayed as she moved around the small office, gathering up paperwork, asking questions that he replied to as quickly and tersely as possible.

A soft wail rose from the other room and he waited for her to respond. When the wail continued for more than ten seconds, he asked, "Aren't you going to check on whoever that is crying?"

"It's Amy, our newborn. And she's hungry. Abby's got to get her bottle ready." She glanced at the simple band of braided leather on her wrist.

"Quite a lot of A's."

With a grin, she said, "This is the A-team. We have Andi, which is me, Abby, Alex, Amy, Aaron, Aspen, and Arnie, the pet hamster." Another glance at her watch, and a few seconds later, the tiny cry was silent as laughter and excited voices filled the air.

Her skin was smooth and pale, not a single freckle marring her milky complexion. And up this close, he doubted that shade of red came out of a bottle. Her eyebrows were the same shade and so was the super fine hair he could see scattered across her arms. Her eyelashes looked to be darker, but behind the glasses, he really couldn't tell.

"Hectic job," he said.

With a roll of her eyes, she said, "Any job that involves anybody under the age of thirteen is hectic."

"What happens after thirteen? Does it become less hectic?"

"No. After thirteen, it just becomes more traumatic. Ever had to deal with a thirteen-year-old girl who was convinced the world was going to stop turning on its axis because the boy from math didn't call the way he said he would?"

"Actually, yes. I have two sisters."

"Then you should already know what happens after thirteen."

Lowering herself to the rolling stool, she asked, "Dizzy?"

Some twenty minutes later, he was ushered out into the relative quiet of the hall, and he had to admit, he agreed with Johnson.

She didn't fit the image of a corporate thief at all.

And she smelled better than he ever would have imagined.

Her mouth, hmm, well, her mouth was probably going to be giving him some sweaty dreams for a night or two. Those naked, pouty lips put only one thing in a man's mind. And the thought had his cock stiffening up like a pike. Just the thought of her putting that mouth on him—

"Enough, McAdams," he muttered, stalking down the hall, absently rubbing his temple. "The girl is a damned embezzler."

About the author:

Shiloh was born in Kentucky and has been reading avidly since she was six. At twelve, she discovered how much fun it was to write when she took a book that didn't end the way she had wanted it to and rewrote the ending. She's been writing ever since.

Shiloh now lives in southern Indiana with her husband and two children. Between her job, her two adorable and demanding children, and equally adorable and demanding husband, she crams writing in between studying and reading and sleeps when time allows.

Shiloh welcomes mail from readers. You can write to her c/o Ellora's Cave Publishing at 1337 Commerce Drive, Suite 13, Stow OH 44224.

Also by Shiloh Walker:

Why an electronic book?

We live in the Information Age—an exciting time in the history of human civilization in which technology rules supreme and continues to progress in leaps and bounds every minute of every hour of every day. For a multitude of reasons, more and more avid literary fans are opting to purchase e-books instead of paperbacks. The question to those not yet initiated to the world of electronic reading is simply: *why?*

1. *Price.* An electronic title at Ellora's Cave Publishing runs anywhere from 40-75% less than the cover price of the <u>exact same title</u> in paperback format. Why? Cold mathematics. It is less expensive to publish an e-book than it is to publish a paperback, so the savings are passed along to the consumer.

2. *Space.* Running out of room to house your paperback books? That is one worry you will never have with electronic novels. For a low one-time cost, you can purchase a handheld computer designed specifically for e-reading purposes. Many e-readers are larger than the average handheld, giving you plenty of screen room. Better yet, hundreds of titles can be stored within your new library—a single microchip. (Please note that Ellora's Cave does not endorse any specific brands. You can check our website at www.ellorascave.com for customer

recommendations we make available to new consumers.)

3. *Mobility.* Because your new library now consists of only a microchip, your entire cache of books can be taken with you wherever you go.

4. *Personal preferences are accounted for.* Are the words you are currently reading too small? Too large? Too...**ANNOYING**? Paperback books cannot be modified according to personal preferences, but e-books can.

5. *Innovation.* The way you read a book is not the only advancement the Information Age has gifted the literary community with. There is also the factor of what you can read. Ellora's Cave Publishing will be introducing a new line of interactive titles that are available in e-book format only.

6. *Instant gratification.* Is it the middle of the night and all the bookstores are closed? Are you tired of waiting days—sometimes weeks—for online and offline bookstores to ship the novels you bought? Ellora's Cave Publishing sells instantaneous downloads 24 hours a day, 7 days a week, 365 days a year. Our e-book delivery system is 100% automated, meaning your order is filled as soon as you pay for it.

Those are a few of the top reasons why electronic novels are displacing paperbacks for many an avid reader. As always, Ellora's Cave Publishing welcomes your questions and comments. We invite you to email us at service@ellorascave.com or write to us directly at: 1337 Commerce Drive, Suite 13, Stow OH 44224.

Printed in the United States
26979LVS00003B/67-273

9 781419 950070